DreamWorks

Trolls

#1

"Hugs & Friends"

PAPERCUTZ

NEW YORK

MORE GREAT GRAPHIC NOVEL SERIES AVAILABLE FROM PAPERCUTZ

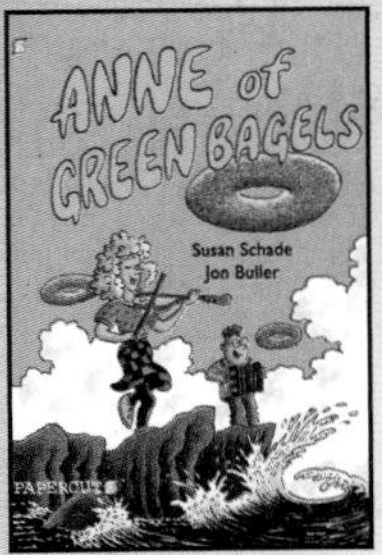
ANNE of GREEN BAGELS
Susan Schade
Jon Buller
PAPERCUTZ
ANNE OF GREEN BAGELS #1

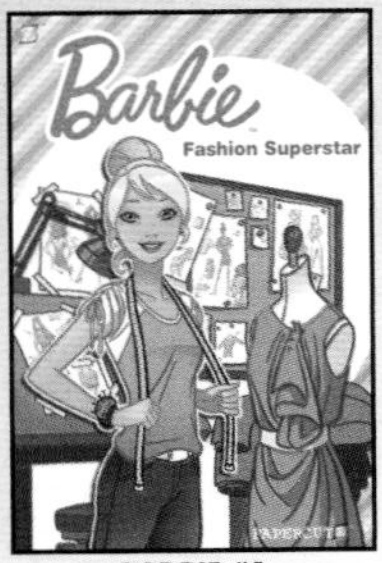
Barbie
Fashion Superstar
PAPERCUTZ
BARBIE #1

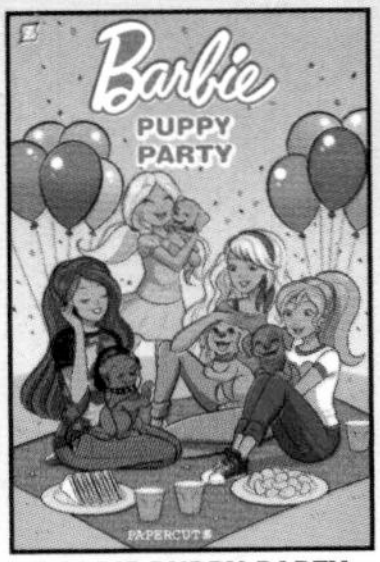
Barbie
PUPPY PARTY
PAPERCUTZ
BARBIE PUPPY PARTY

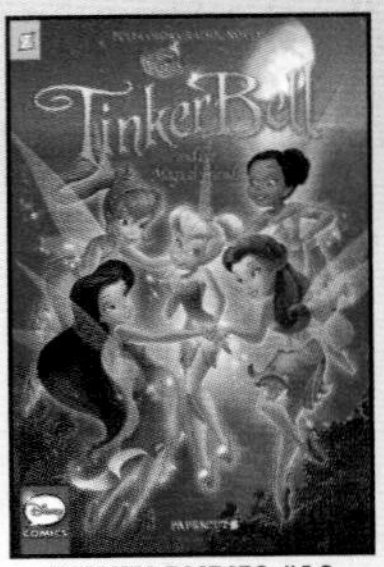
Tinker Bell
PAPERCUTZ
DISNEY FAIRIES #18

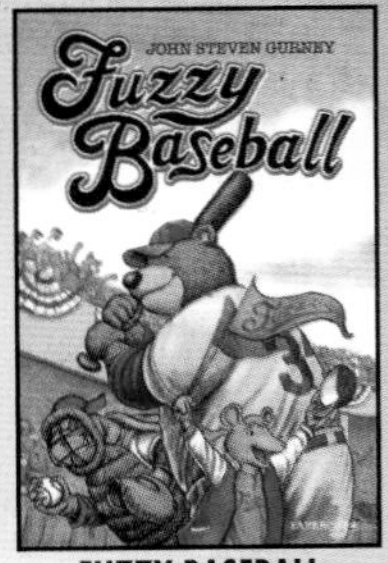
JOHN STEVEN GURNEY
Fuzzy Baseball
FUZZY BASEBALL

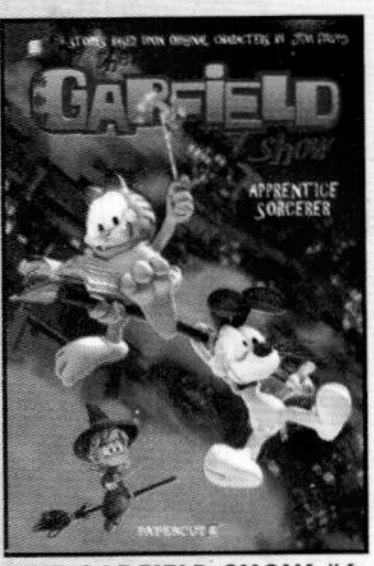
GARFIELD
APPRENTICE SORCERER
PAPERCUTZ
THE GARFIELD SHOW #6

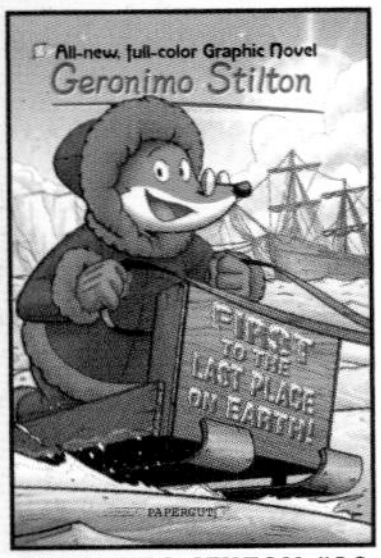
All-new, full-color Graphic Novel
Geronimo Stilton
FIRST TO THE LAST PLACE ON EARTH!
PAPERCUTZ
GERONIMO STILTON #18

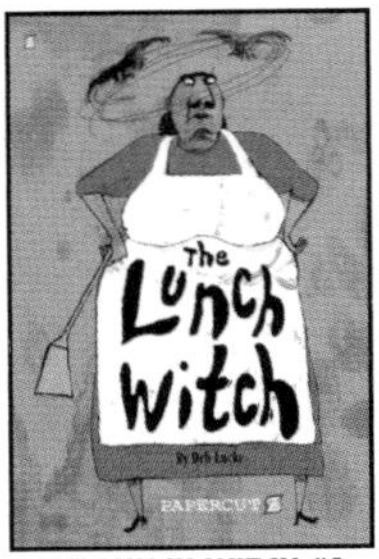
The Lunch Witch
By Deb Lucke
PAPERCUTZ
THE LUNCH WITCH #1

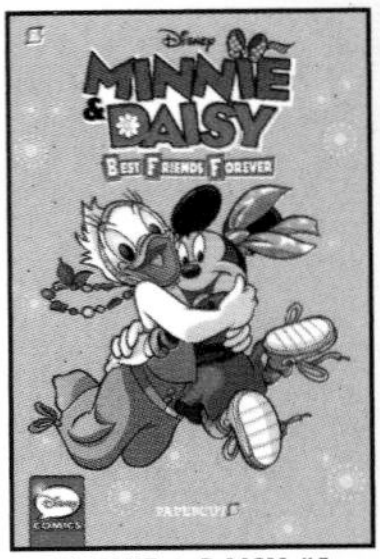
Disney
MINNIE & DAISY
BEST FRIENDS FOREVER
PAPERCUTZ
MINNIE & DAISY #1

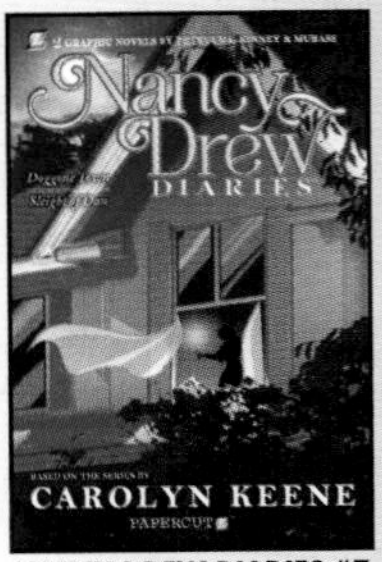
Nancy Drew
DIARIES
CAROLYN KEENE
PAPERCUTZ
NANCY DREW DIARIES #7

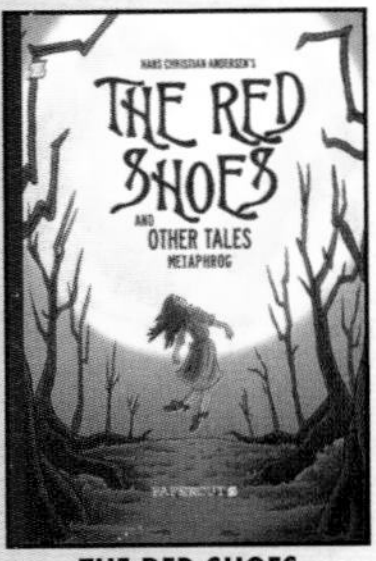
HANS CHRISTIAN ANDERSEN'S
THE RED SHOES
AND OTHER TALES
METAPHROG
PAPERCUTZ
THE RED SHOES

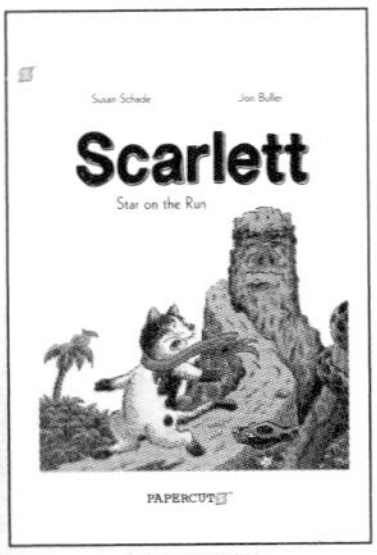
Susan Schade
Jon Buller
Scarlett
Star on the Run
PAPERCUTZ
SCARLETT

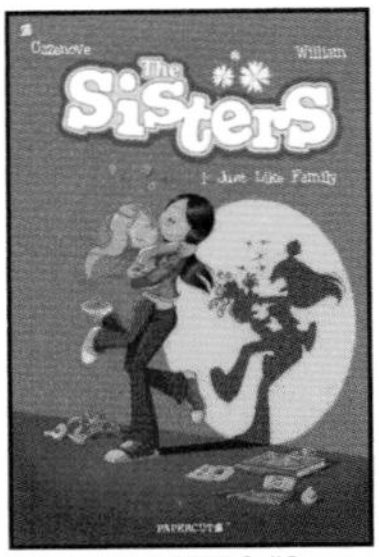
Cazenove
William
The Sisters
PAPERCUTZ
THE SISTERS #1

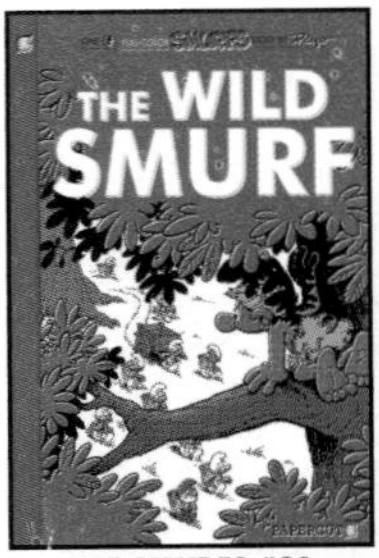
THE WILD SMURF
PAPERCUTZ
THE SMURFS #21

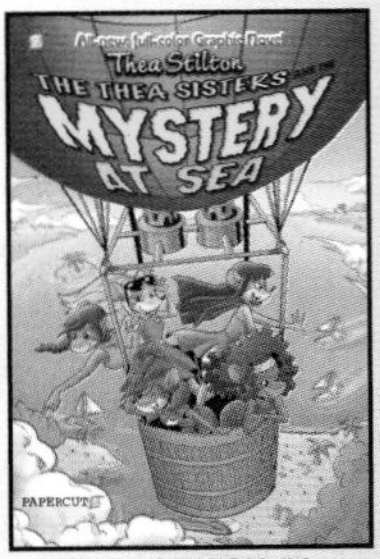
Thea Stilton
THE THEA SISTERS
MYSTERY AT SEA
PAPERCUTZ
THEA STILTON #6

THE SMURFS, MINNIE & DAISY, DISNEY FAIRIES, THE GARFIELD SHOW, BARBIE and TROLLS graphic novels are available for $7.99 in paperback, and $12.99 in hardcover. GERONIMO STILTON and THEA STILTON graphic novels are available for $9.99 in hardcover only. FUZZY BASEBALL and NANCY DREW DIARIES graphic novels are available for $9.99 in paperback only. THE LUNCH WITCH, SCARLETT, and ANNE OF GREEN BAGELS graphic novels are available for $14.99 in paperback only. THE RED SHOES graphic novel is available for $12.99 in hardcover only.
Available from booksellers everywhere. You can also order online from www.papercutz.com. Or call 1-800-886-1223, Monday through Friday, 9–5 EST. MC, Visa, and AmEx accepted. To order by mail, please add $4.00 for postage and handling for first book ordered, $1.00 for each additional book and make check payable to NBM Publishing.
Send to: Papercutz, 160 Broadway, Suite 700, East Wing, New York, NY 10038.

THE SMURFS, THE GARFIELD SHOW, BARBIE, TROLLS, GERONIMO STILTON, THEA STILTON, FUZZY BASEBALL, THE LUNCH WITCH, NANCY DREW DIARIES, THE RED SHOES, ANNE OF GREEN BAGELS, and SCARLETT graphic novels are also available wherever e-books are sold.

DreamWorks

Trolls

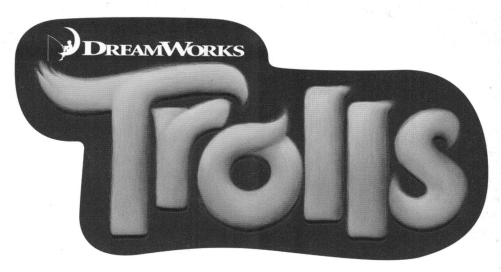

TABLE OF CONTENTS

#1 DreamWorks Trolls

"Hugs & Friends"

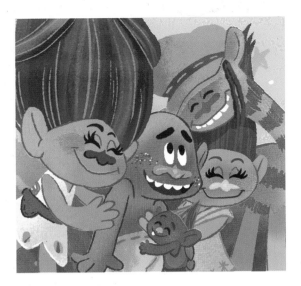

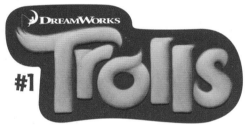

Dave Scheidt – Trolls Writer
Tini Howard – Bergens Writer
Kathryn Hudson – Artist and Colorist
Tom Orzechowski – Letterer

Dawn Guzzo – Design/Production
Rachel Pinnelas – Production Coordinator
Bethany Bryan – Editor
Jeff Whitman – Assistant Managing Editor
Jim Salicrup
Editor-in-Chief

ISBN: 978-1-62991-583-8 paperback edition
ISBN: 978-1-62991-584-5 hardcover edition

Papercutz books may be purchased for business or promotional use.
For information on bulk purchases please contact Macmillan Corporate and Premium Sales Department at (800) 221-7945 x5442.

Printed in Canada
September 2016 by Marquis

Distributed by Macmillan
First Printing

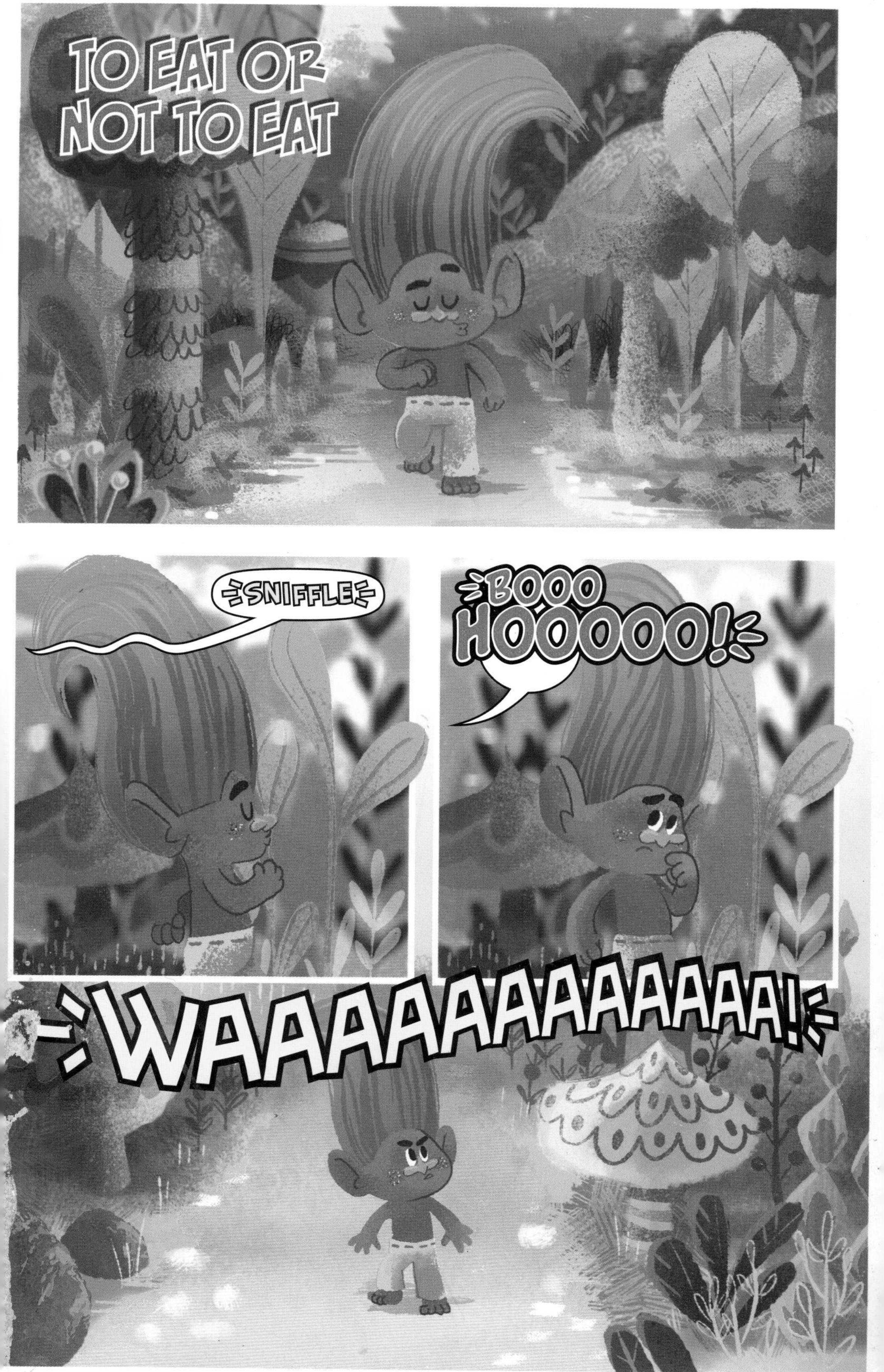
TO EAT OR NOT TO EAT
SNIFFLE
BOOO HOOOOOO!
WAAAAAAAAAAAA!

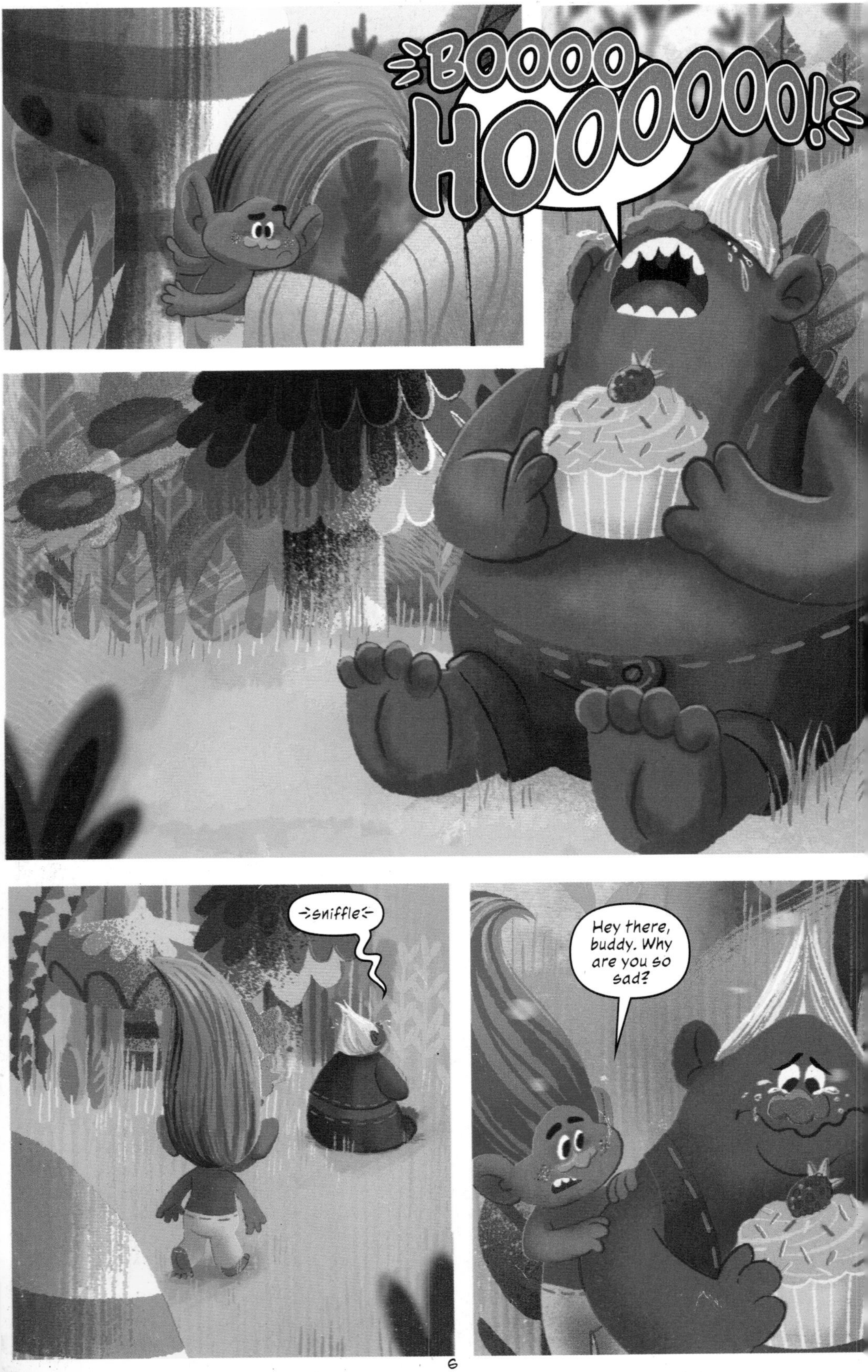

BOOOO HOOOOOO!
sniffle
Hey there, buddy. Why are you so sad?

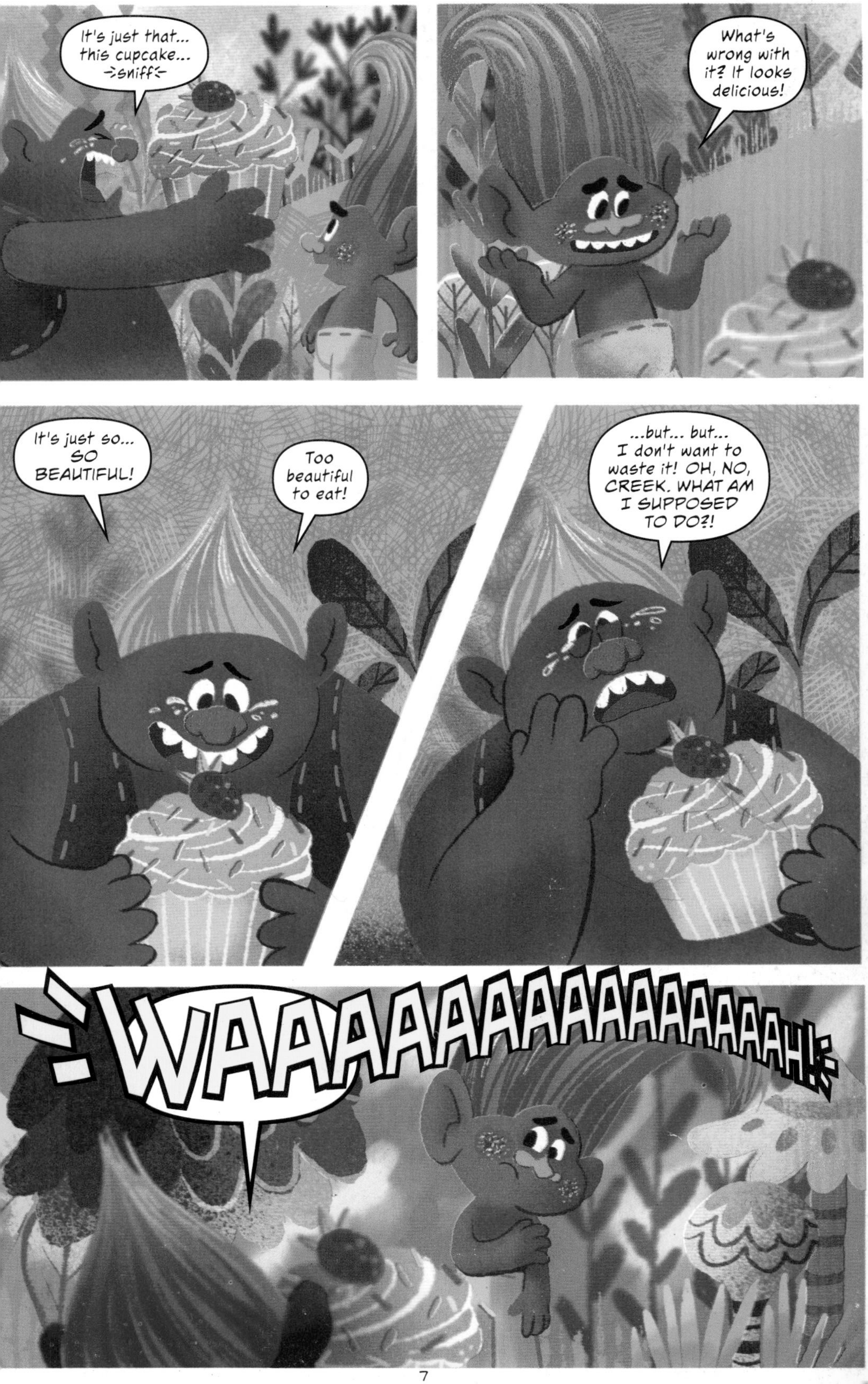
It's just that... this cupcake... ~sniff~
What's wrong with it? It looks delicious!
It's just so... SO BEAUTIFUL!
Too beautiful to eat!
...but... but... I don't want to waste it! OH, NO, CREEK. WHAT AM I SUPPOSED TO DO?!
WAAAAAAAAAAAAAAAAH!

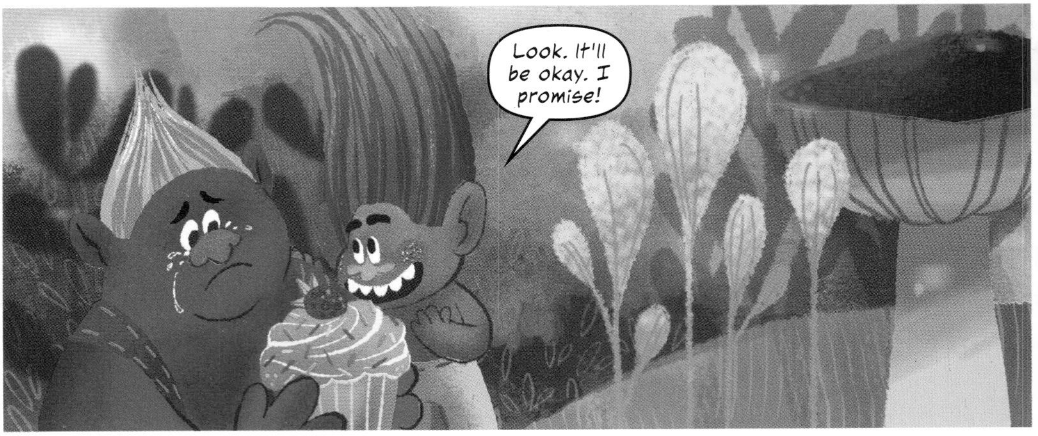
Look. It'll be okay. I promise!

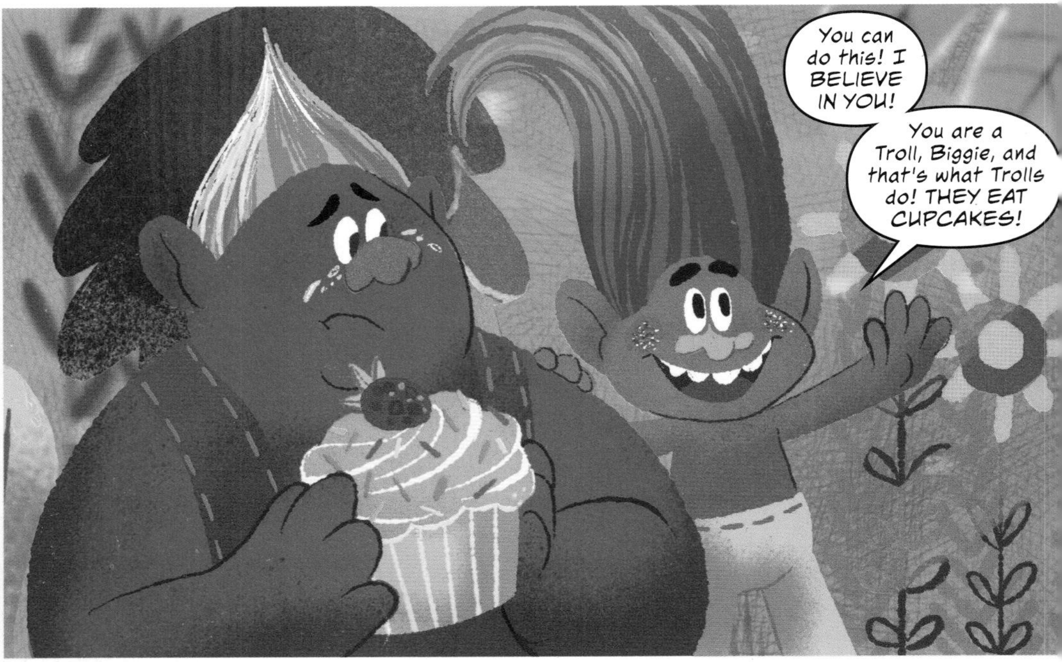
You can do this! I BELIEVE IN YOU!
You are a Troll, Biggie, and that's what Trolls do! THEY EAT CUPCAKES!

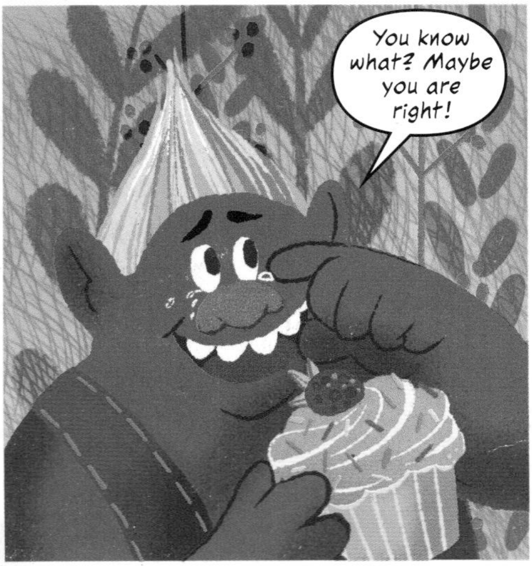
You know what? Maybe you are right!

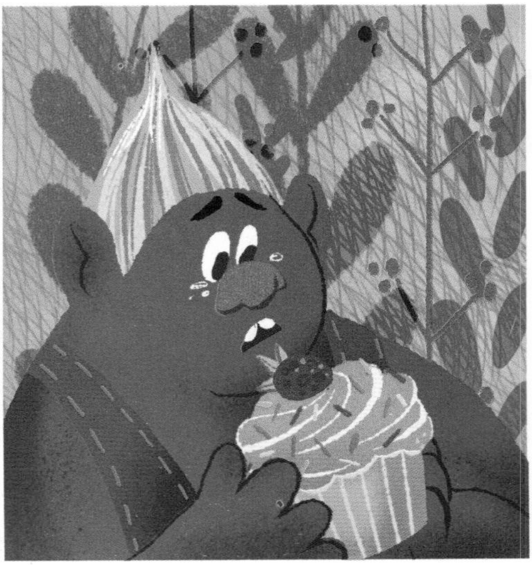

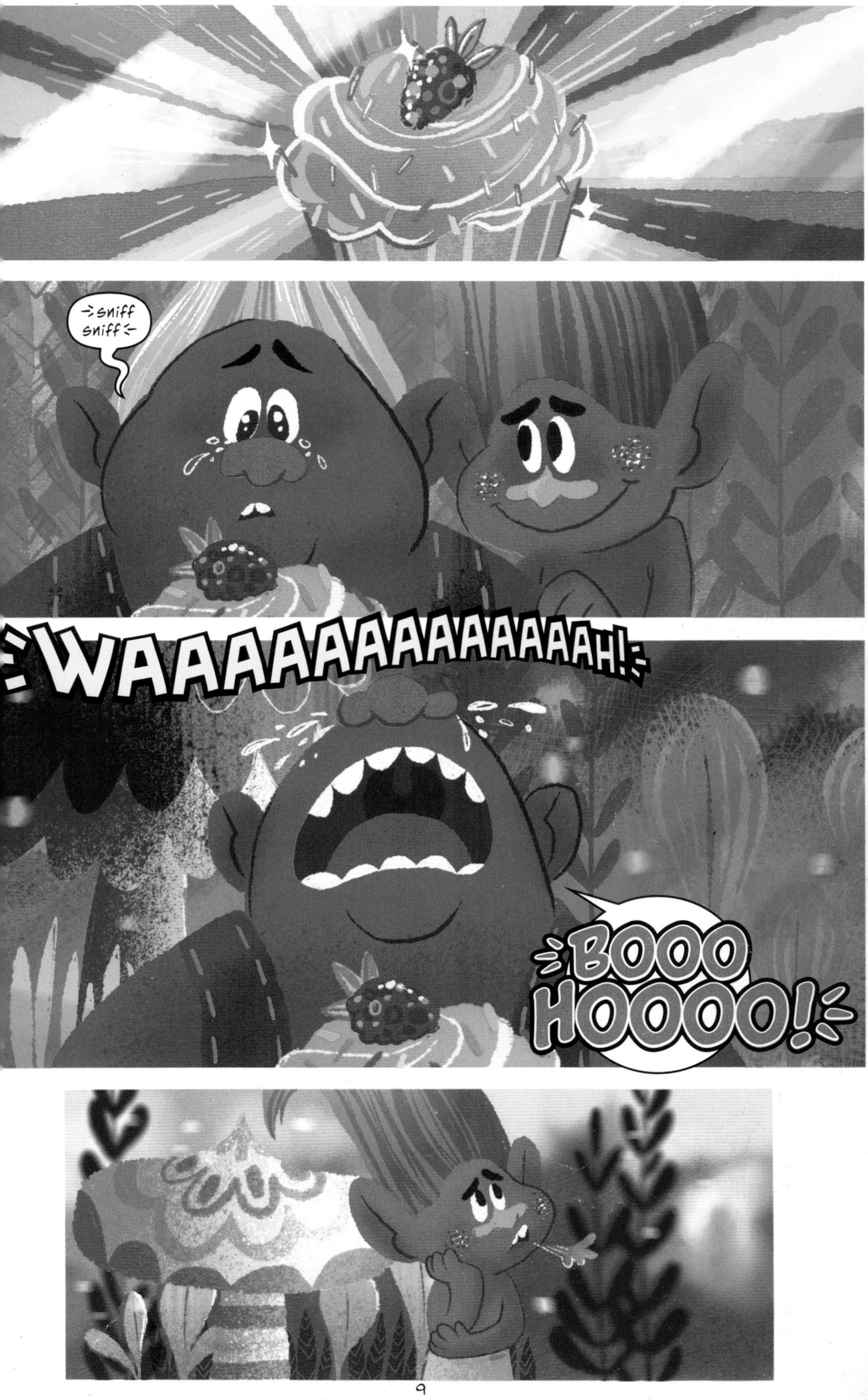
sniff sniff
WAAAAAAAAAAAAAH!
BOOO HOOOOO!

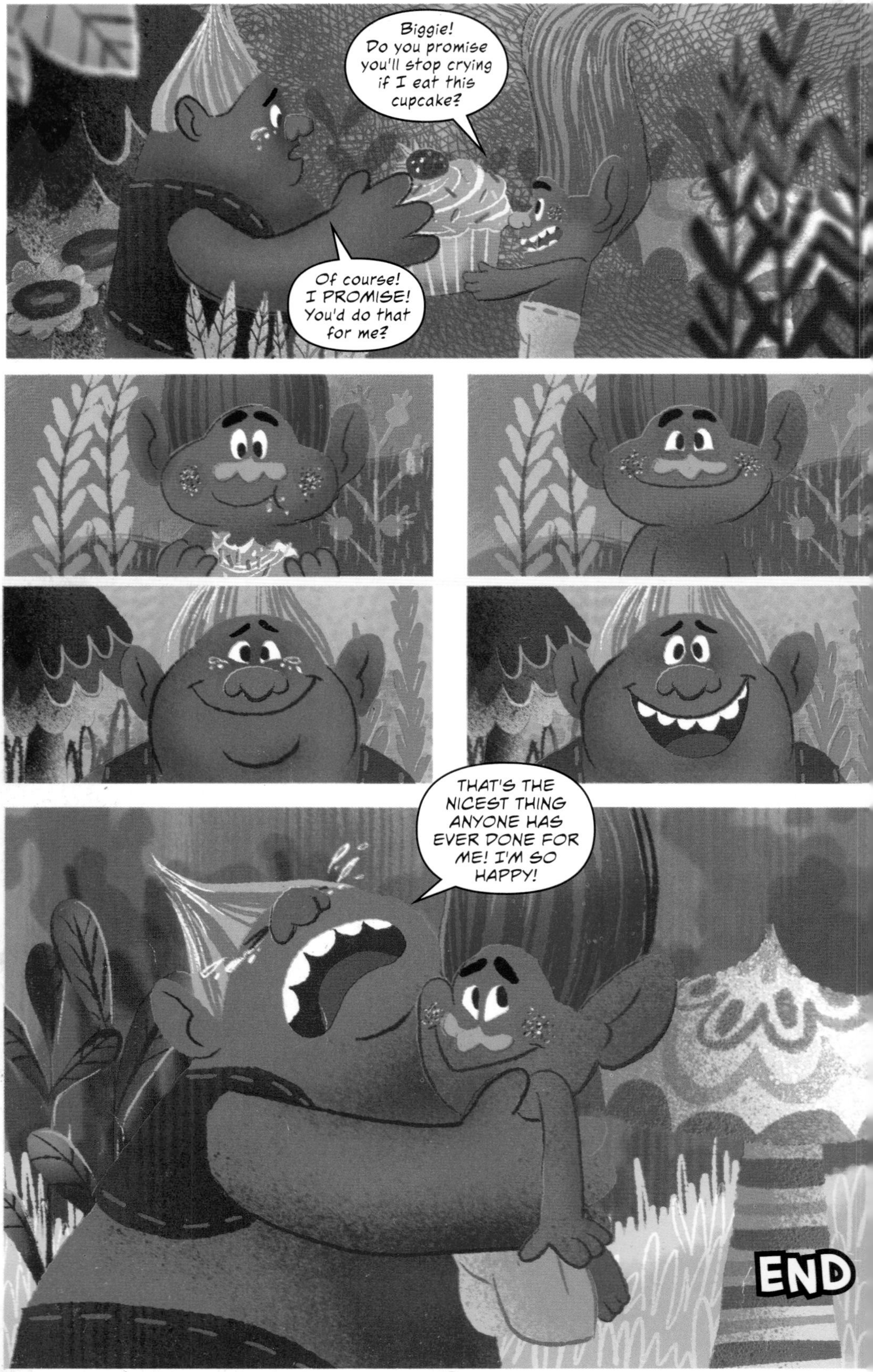
Biggie!
Do you promise you'll stop crying if I eat this cupcake?
Of course! I PROMISE! You'd do that for me?
THAT'S THE NICEST THING ANYONE HAS EVER DONE FOR ME! I'M SO HAPPY!
END

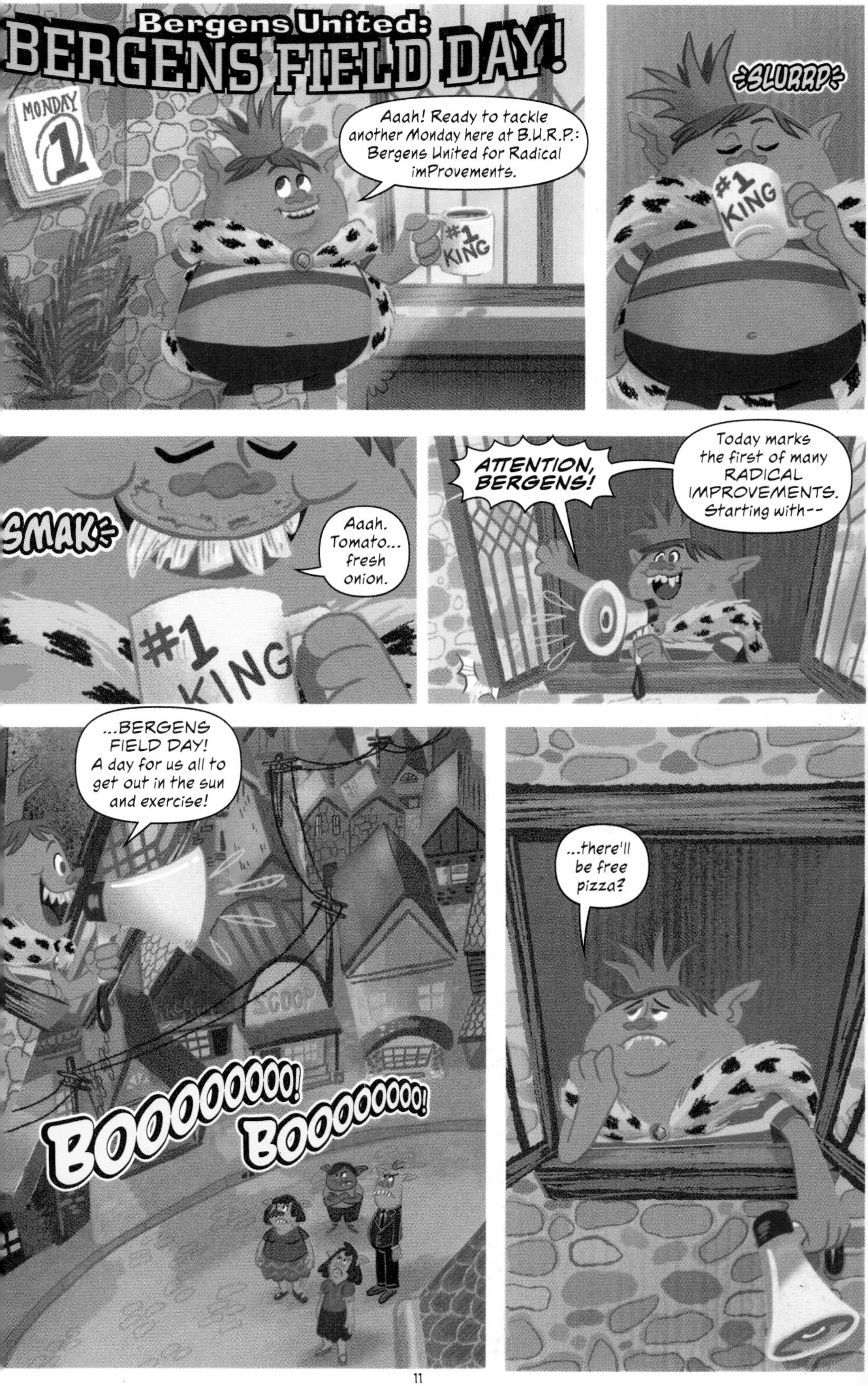
Bergens United:
BERGENS FIELD DAY!
MONDAY 1
Aaah! Ready to tackle another Monday here at B.U.R.P.: Bergens United for Radical imProvements.
#1 KING
SLURRP
#1 KING
SMAK
Aaah. Tomato... fresh onion.
#1 KING
ATTENTION, BERGENS!
Today marks the first of many RADICAL IMPROVEMENTS. Starting with--
...BERGENS FIELD DAY! A day for us all to get out in the sun and exercise!
SCOOP
BOOOOOOOO! BOOOOOOOO!
...there'll be free pizza?

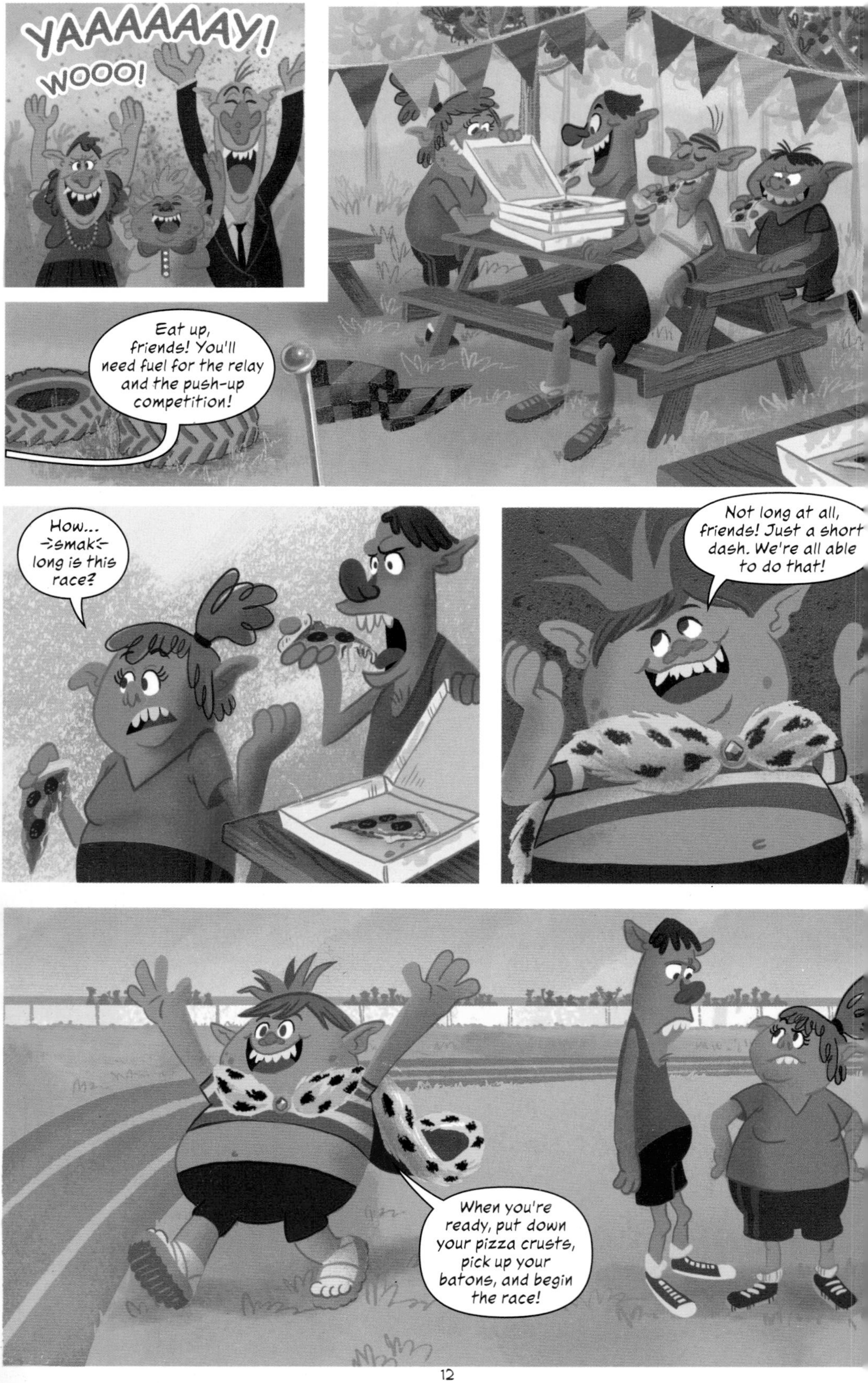
YAAAAAAY!
WOOO!
Eat up, friends! You'll need fuel for the relay and the push-up competition!
How... -smak- long is this race?
Not long at all, friends! Just a short dash. We're all able to do that!
When you're ready, put down your pizza crusts, pick up your batons, and begin the race!

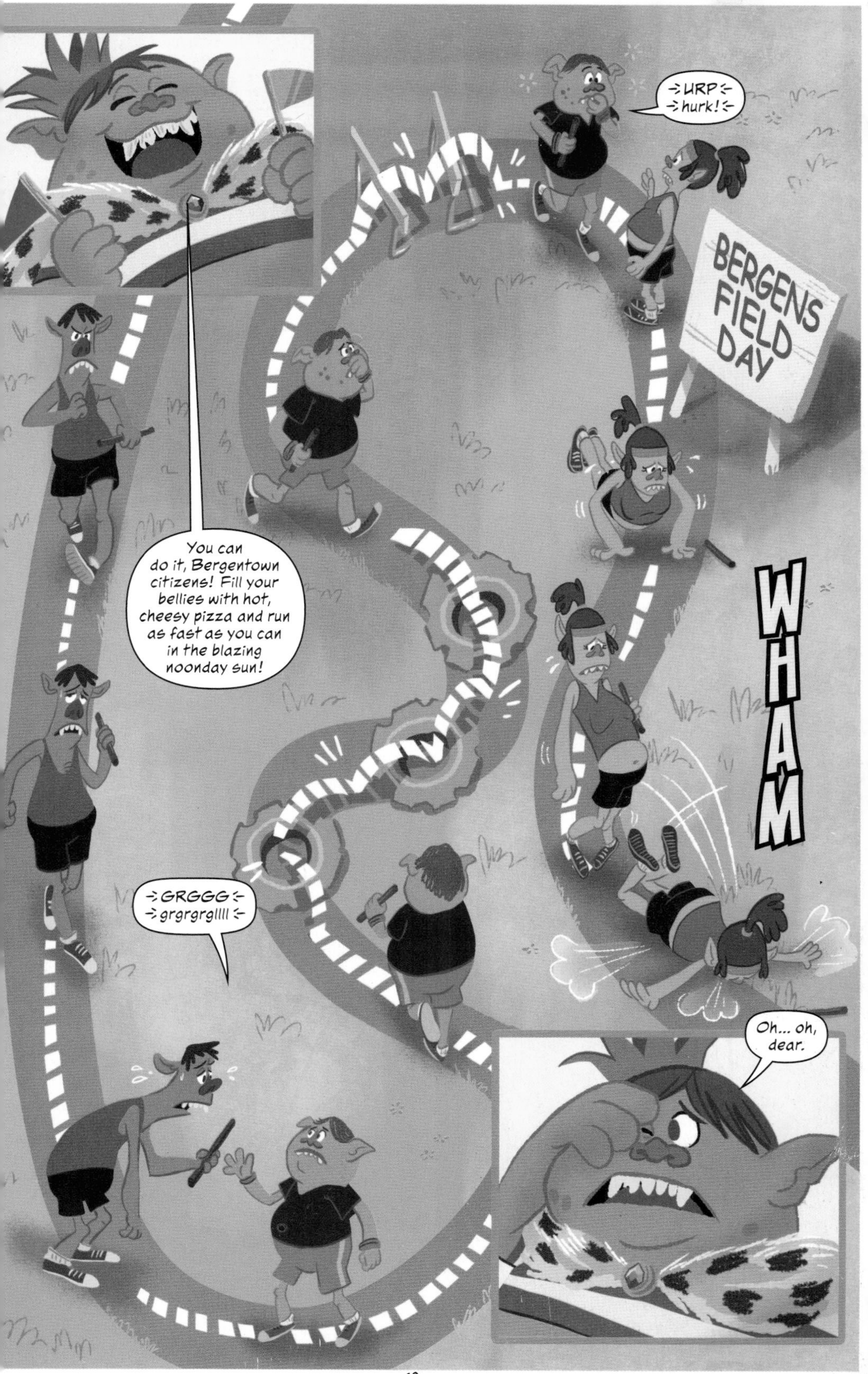
URP
hurk!
BERGENS FIELD DAY
You can do it, Bergentown citizens! Fill your bellies with hot, cheesy pizza and run as fast as you can in the blazing noonday sun!
WHAM
GRGGG
grgrgrglll
Oh... oh, dear.

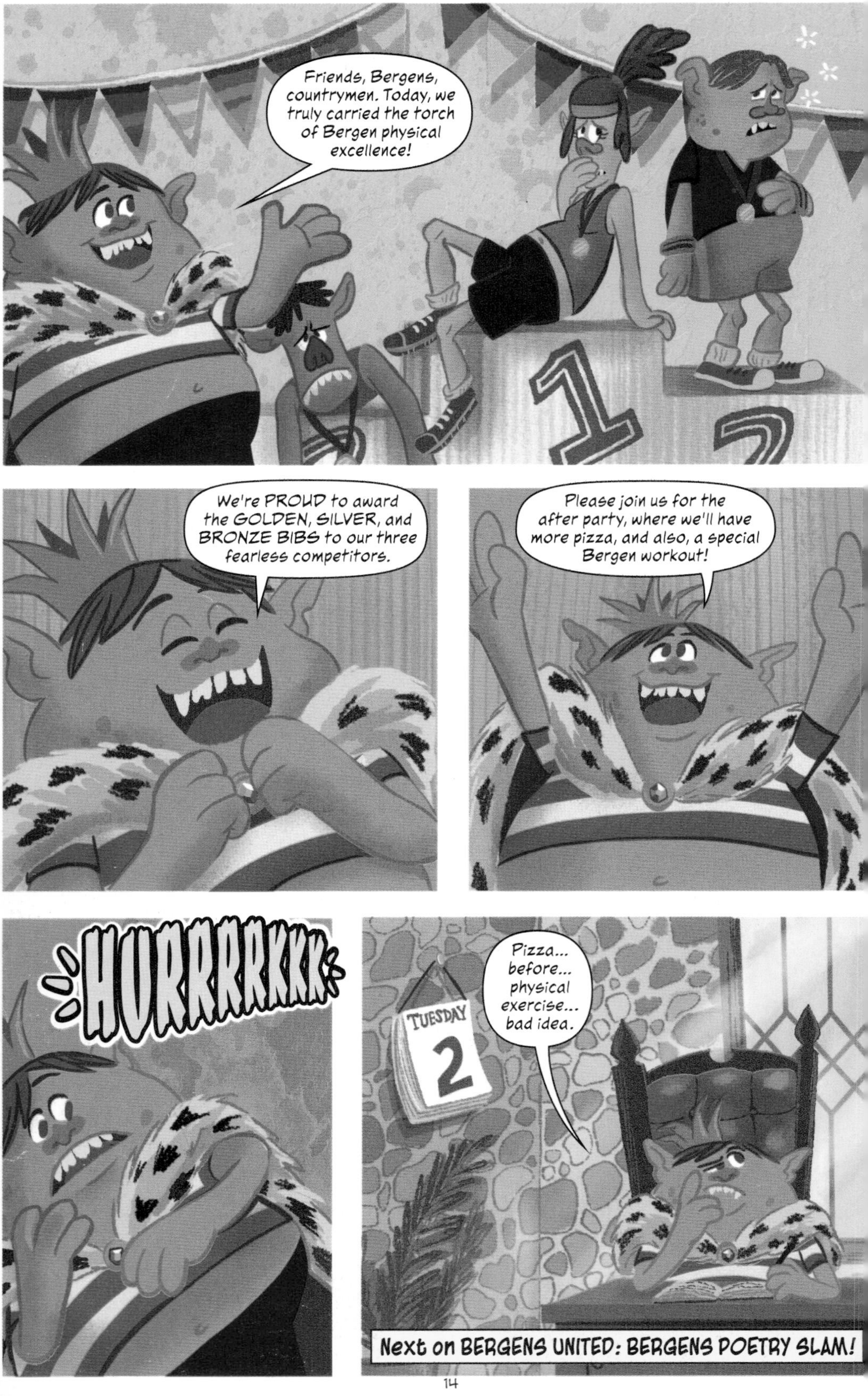
Friends, Bergens, countrymen. Today, we truly carried the torch of Bergen physical excellence!
We're PROUD to award the GOLDEN, SILVER, and BRONZE BIBS to our three fearless competitors.
Please join us for the after party, where we'll have more pizza, and also, a special Bergen workout!
HURRRRKKK
TUESDAY
2
Pizza... before... physical exercise... bad idea.
Next on BERGENS UNITED: BERGENS POETRY SLAM!

PAINT HOW YOU FEEL

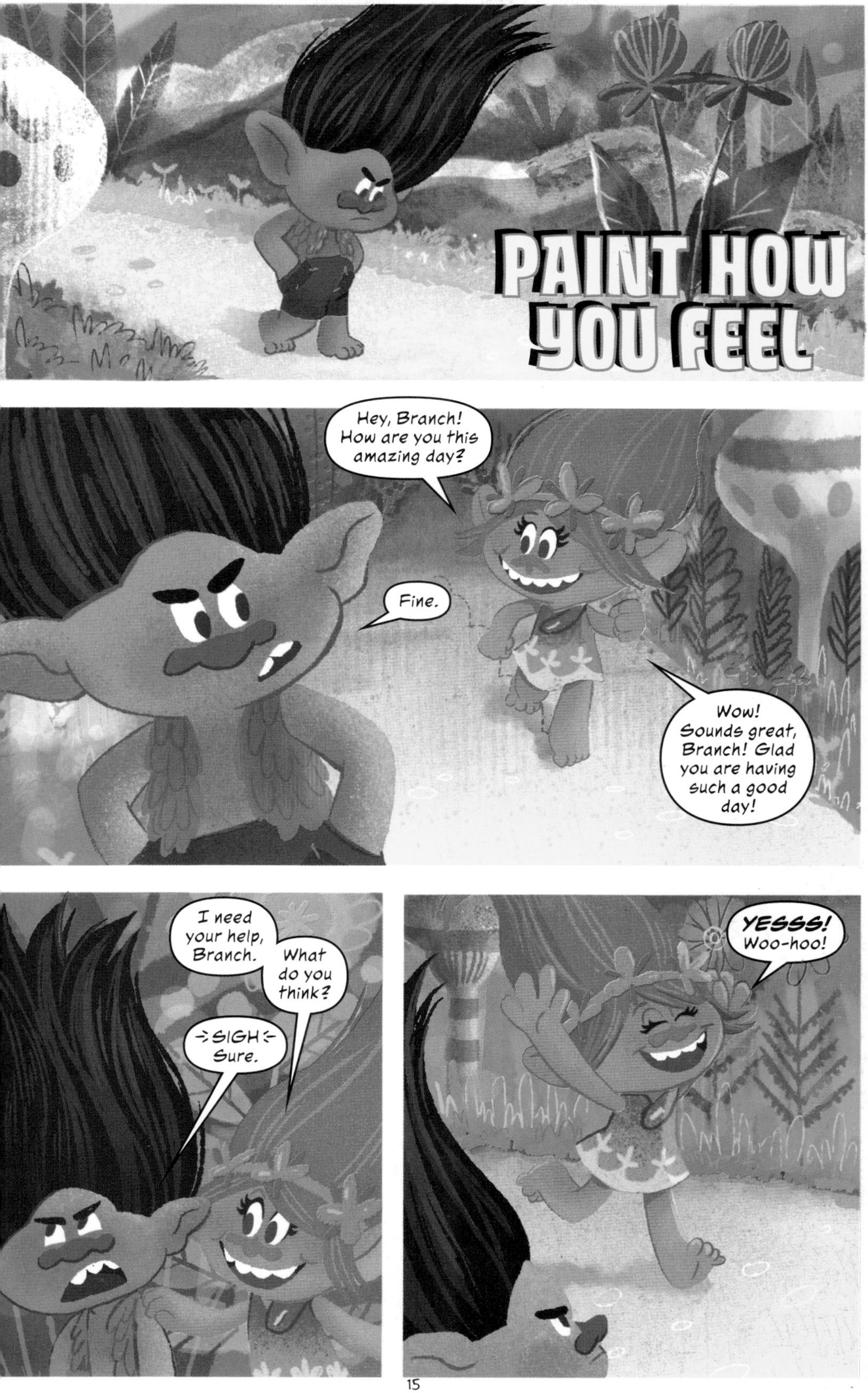
Hey, Branch! How are you this amazing day?
Fine.
Wow! Sounds great, Branch! Glad you are having such a good day!
I need your help, Branch.
What do you think?
SIGH Sure.
YESSS! Woo-hoo!

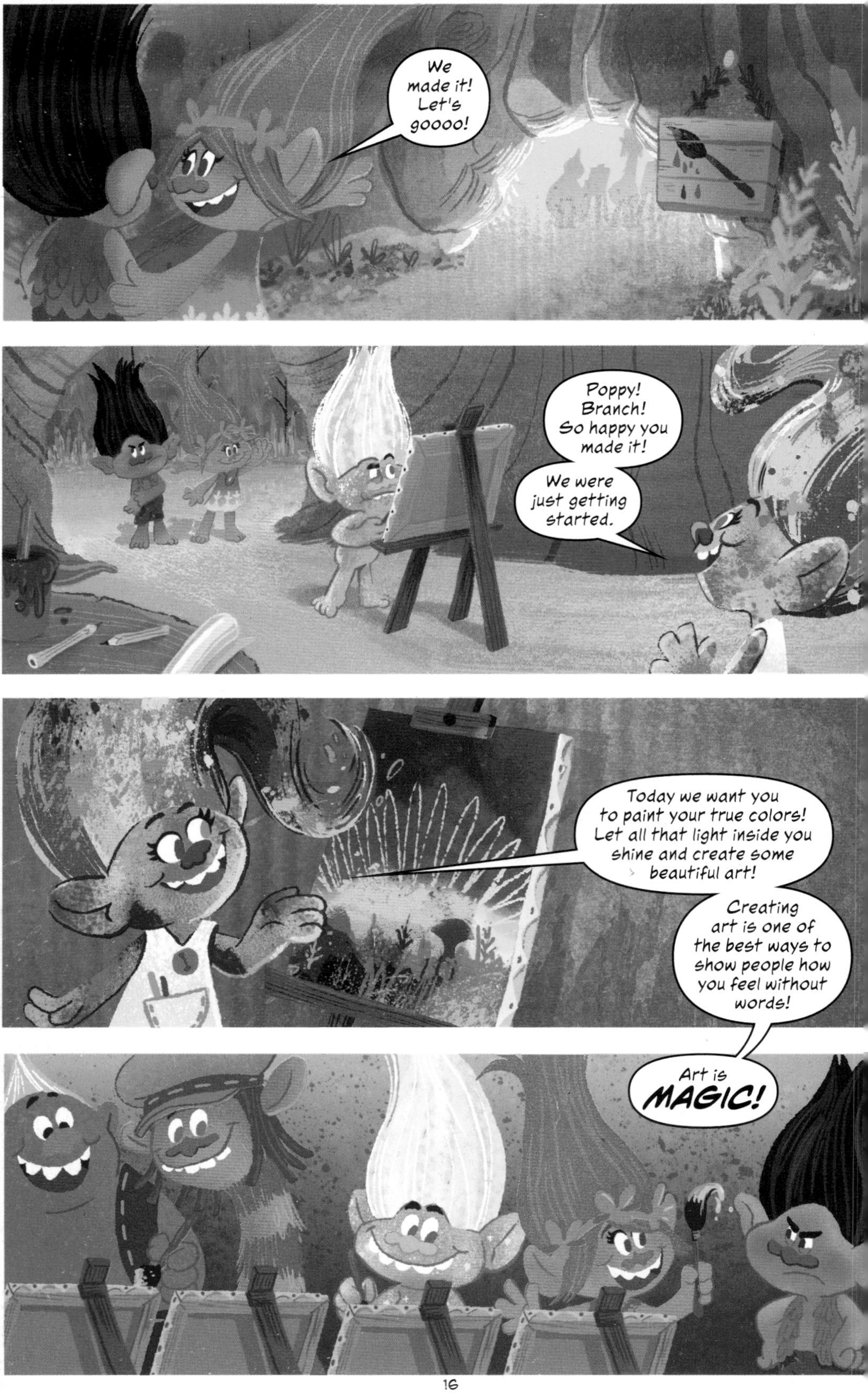
We made it! Let's goooo!
Poppy! Branch! So happy you made it!
We were just getting started.
Today we want you to paint your true colors! Let all that light inside you shine and create some beautiful art!
Creating art is one of the best ways to show people how you feel without words!
Art is MAGIC!

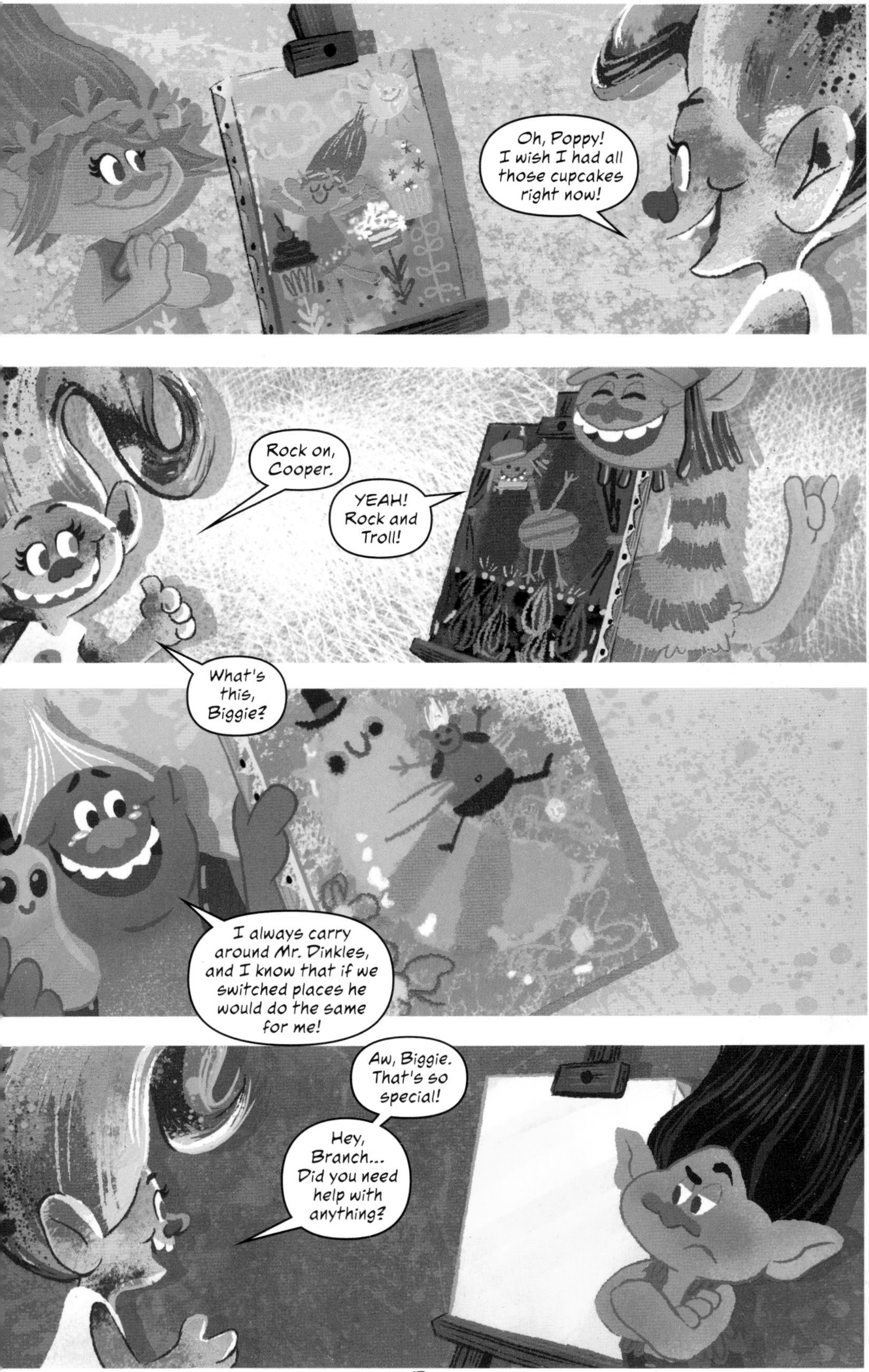
Oh, Poppy! I wish I had all those cupcakes right now!
Rock on, Cooper.
YEAH! Rock and Troll!
What's this, Biggie?
I always carry around Mr. Dinkles, and I know that if we switched places he would do the same for me!
Aw, Biggie. That's so special!
Hey, Branch... Did you need help with anything?

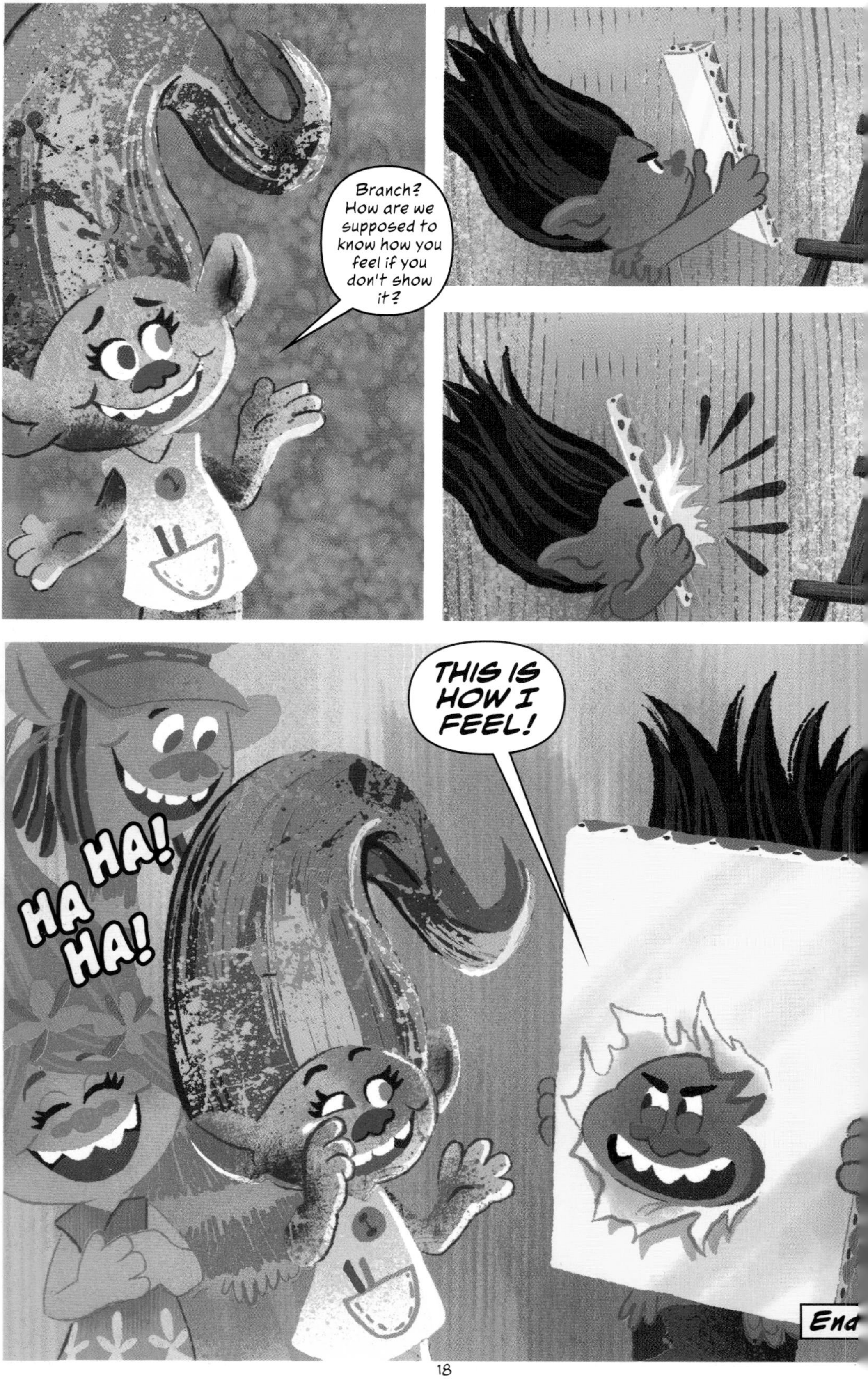
Branch? How are we supposed to know how you feel if you don't show it?
THIS IS HOW I FEEL!
HA HA! HA HA!
End

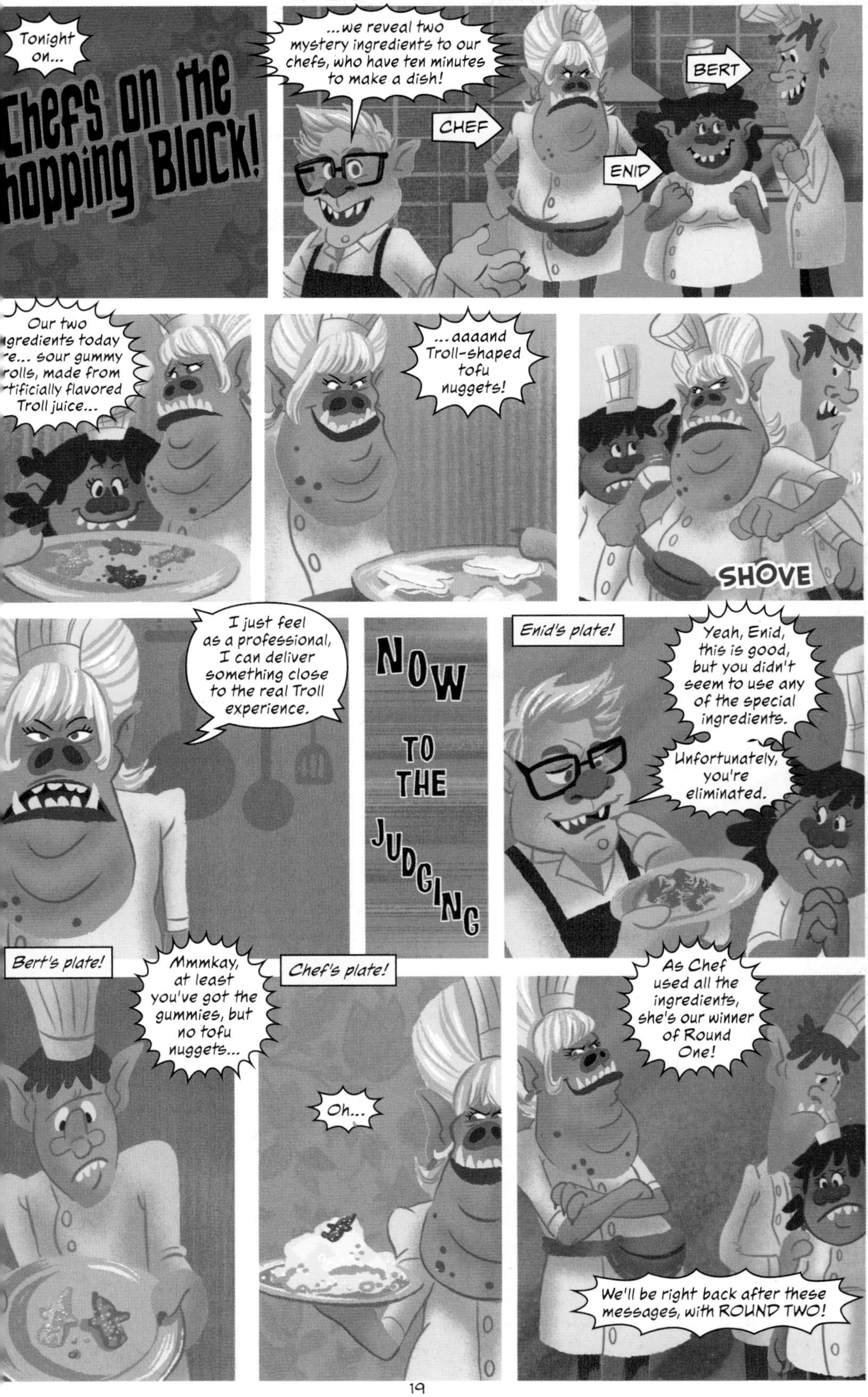
Tonight on...
Chefs on the hopping BLOCK!
...we reveal two mystery ingredients to our chefs, who have ten minutes to make a dish!
CHEF
BERT
ENID
Our two gredients today re... sour gummy rolls, made from tificially flavored Troll juice...
...aaaand Troll-shaped tofu nuggets!
SHOVE
I just feel as a professional, I can deliver something close to the real Troll experience.
NOW TO THE JUDGING
Enid's plate!
Yeah, Enid, this is good, but you didn't seem to use any of the special ingredients.
Unfortunately, you're eliminated.
Bert's plate!
Mmmkay, at least you've got the gummies, but no tofu nuggets...
Chef's plate!
Oh...
As Chef used all the ingredients, she's our winner of Round One!
We'll be right back after these messages, with ROUND TWO!

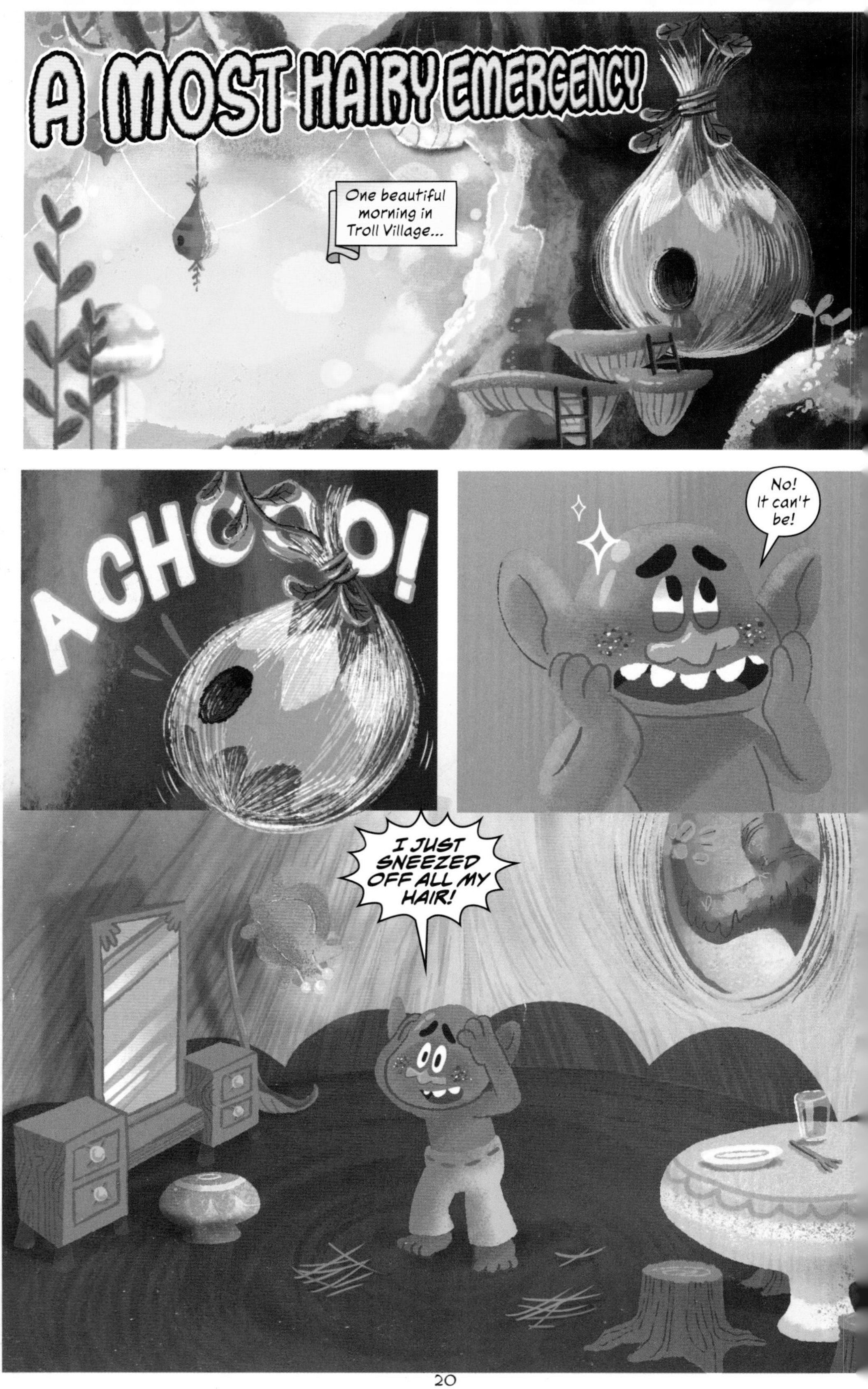
A MOST HAIRY EMERGENCY
One beautiful morning in Troll Village...
ACHOO!
No! It can't be!
I JUST SNEEZED OFF ALL MY HAIR!

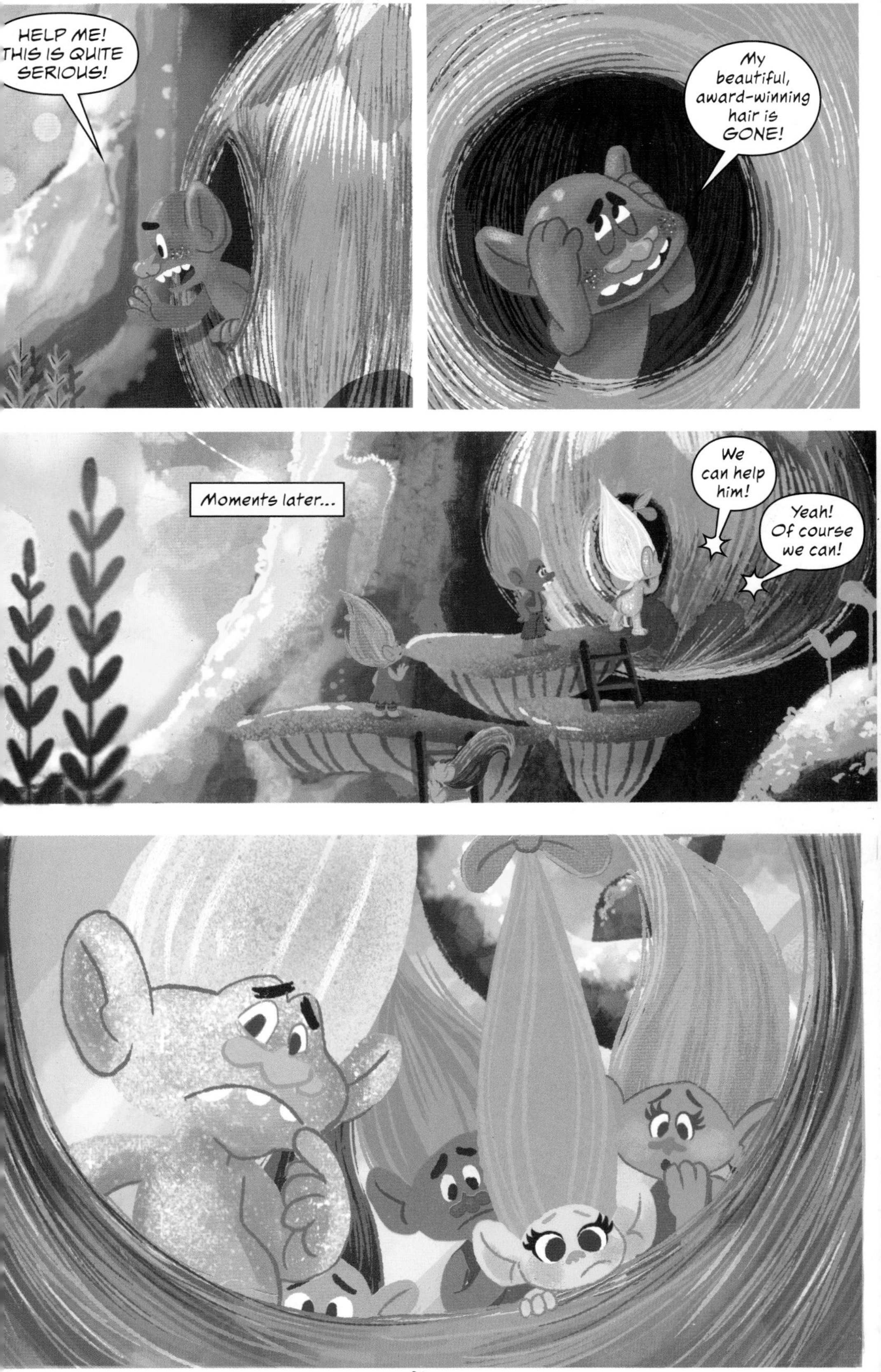
HELP ME! THIS IS QUITE SERIOUS!
My beautiful, award-winning hair is GONE!
Moments later...
We can help him!
Yeah! Of course we can!

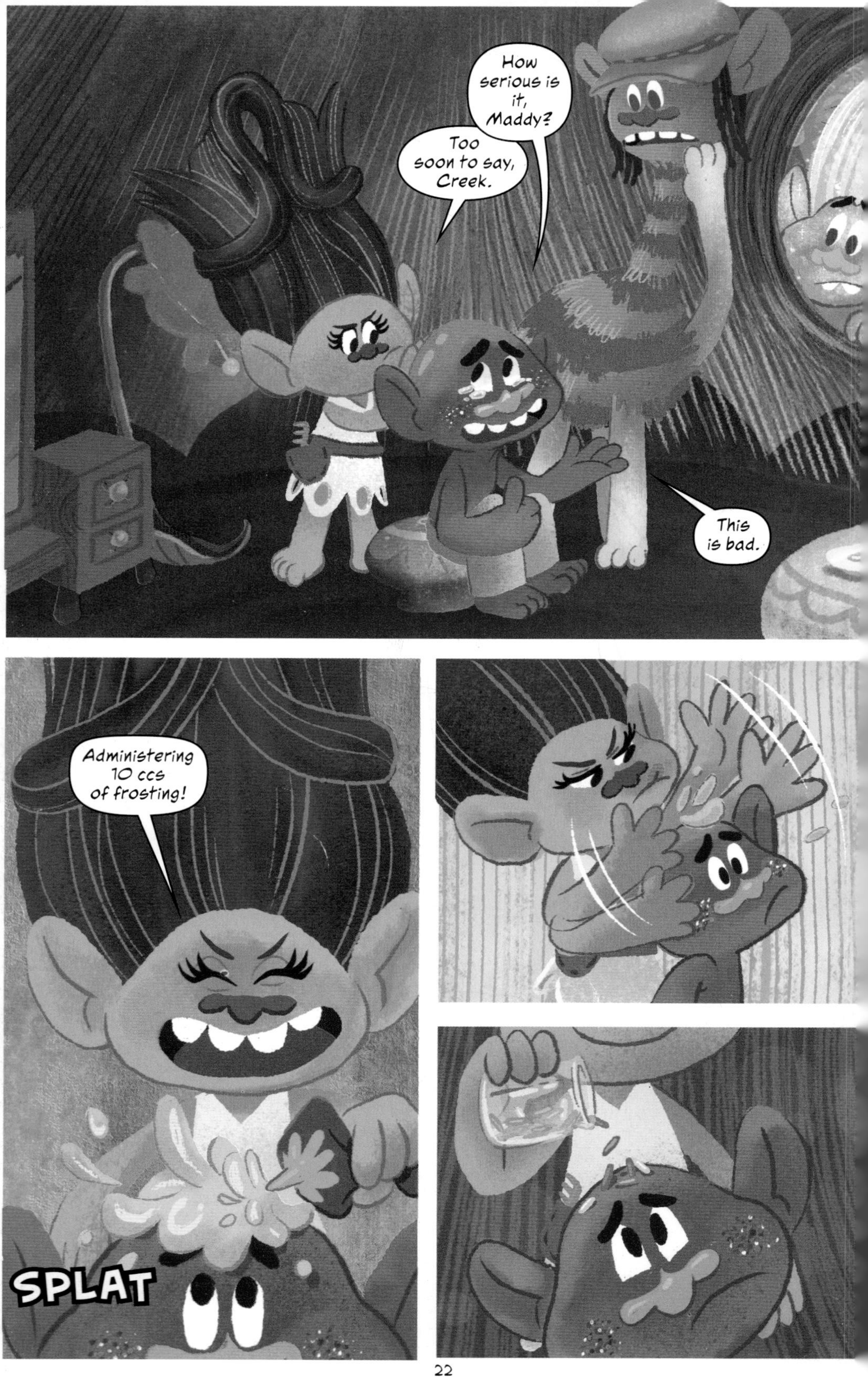
How serious is it, Maddy?
Too soon to say, Creek.
This is bad.
Administering 10 ccs of frosting!
SPLAT

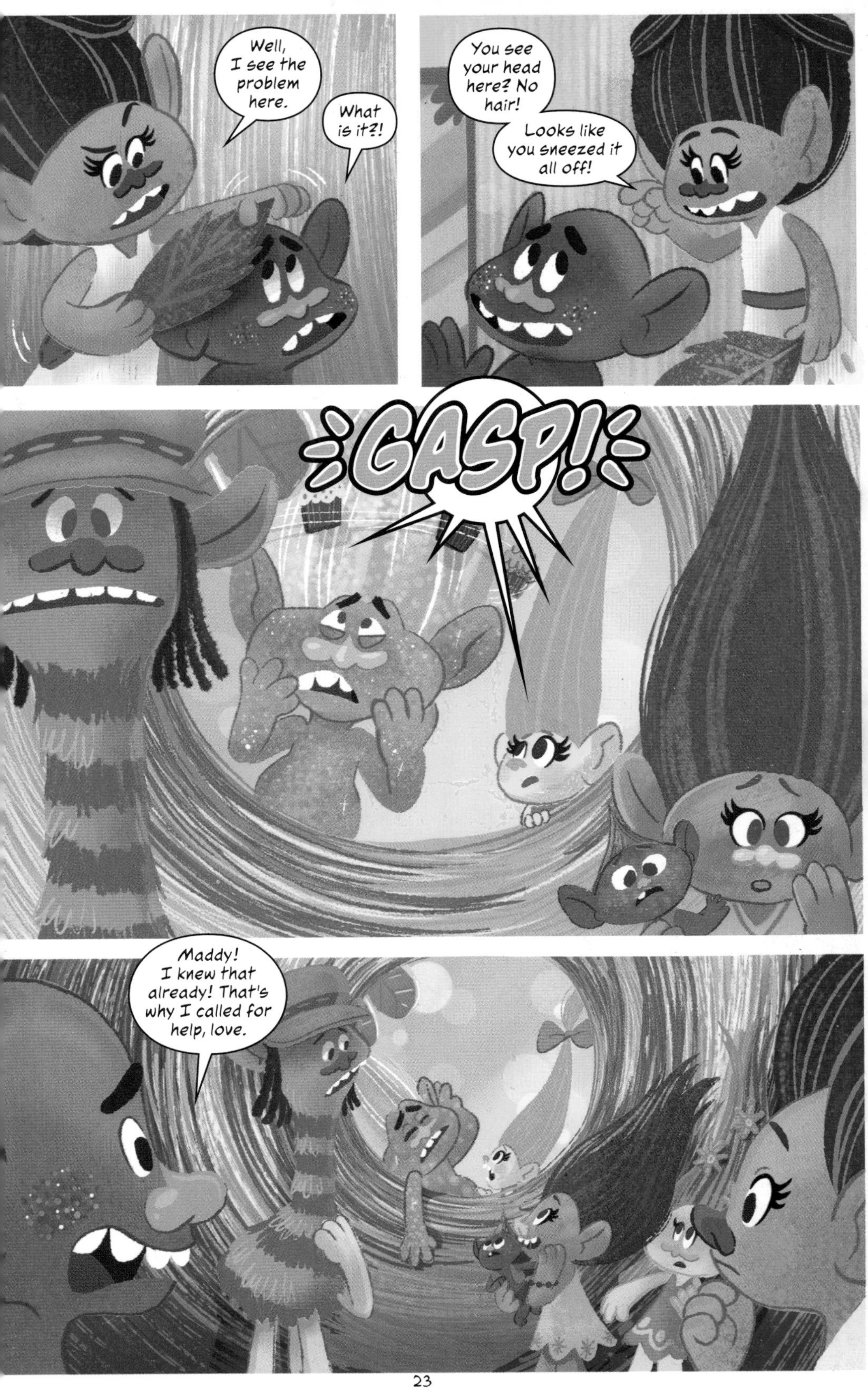
Well, I see the problem here.
What is it?!
You see your head here? No hair!
Looks like you sneezed it all off!
GASP!
Maddy! I knew that already! That's why I called for help, love.

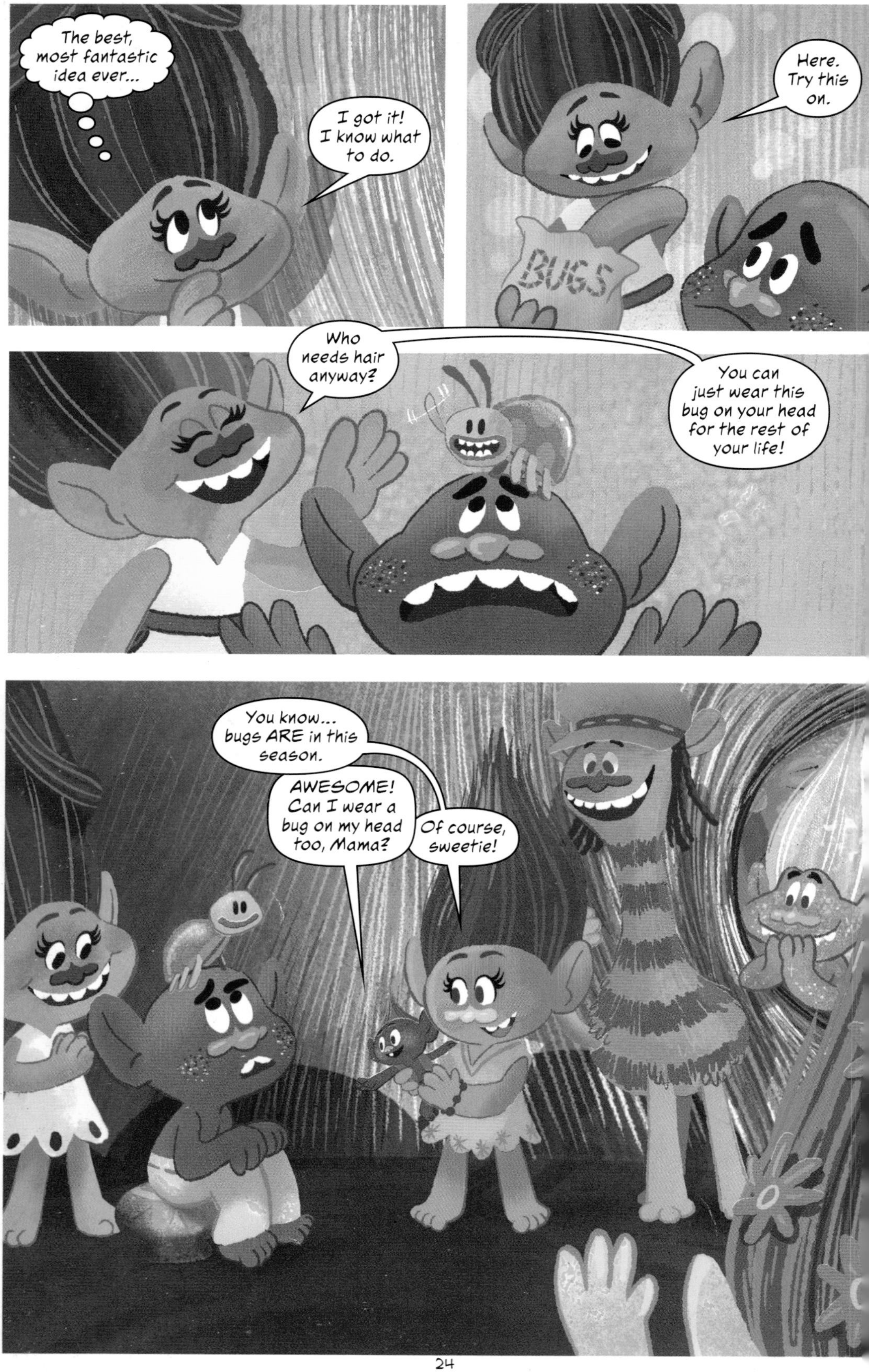
The best, most fantastic idea ever...
I got it! I know what to do.
Here. Try this on.
BUGS
Who needs hair anyway?
You can just wear this bug on your head for the rest of your life!
You know... bugs ARE in this season.
AWESOME! Can I wear a bug on my head too, Mama?
Of course, sweetie!

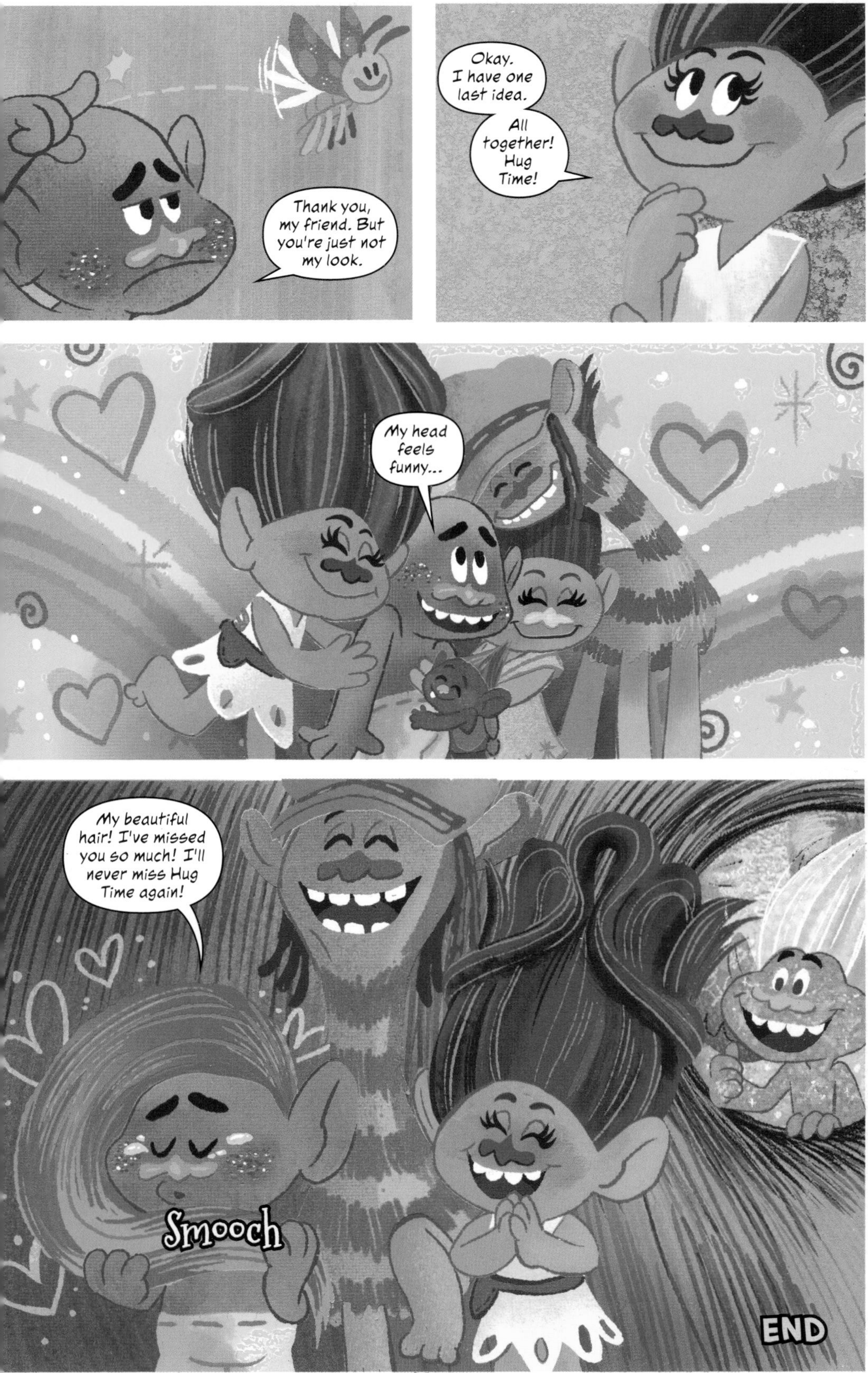
Thank you, my friend. But you're just not my look.
Okay. I have one last idea.
All together! Hug Time!
My head feels funny...
My beautiful hair! I've missed you so much! I'll never miss Hug Time again!
Smooch
END

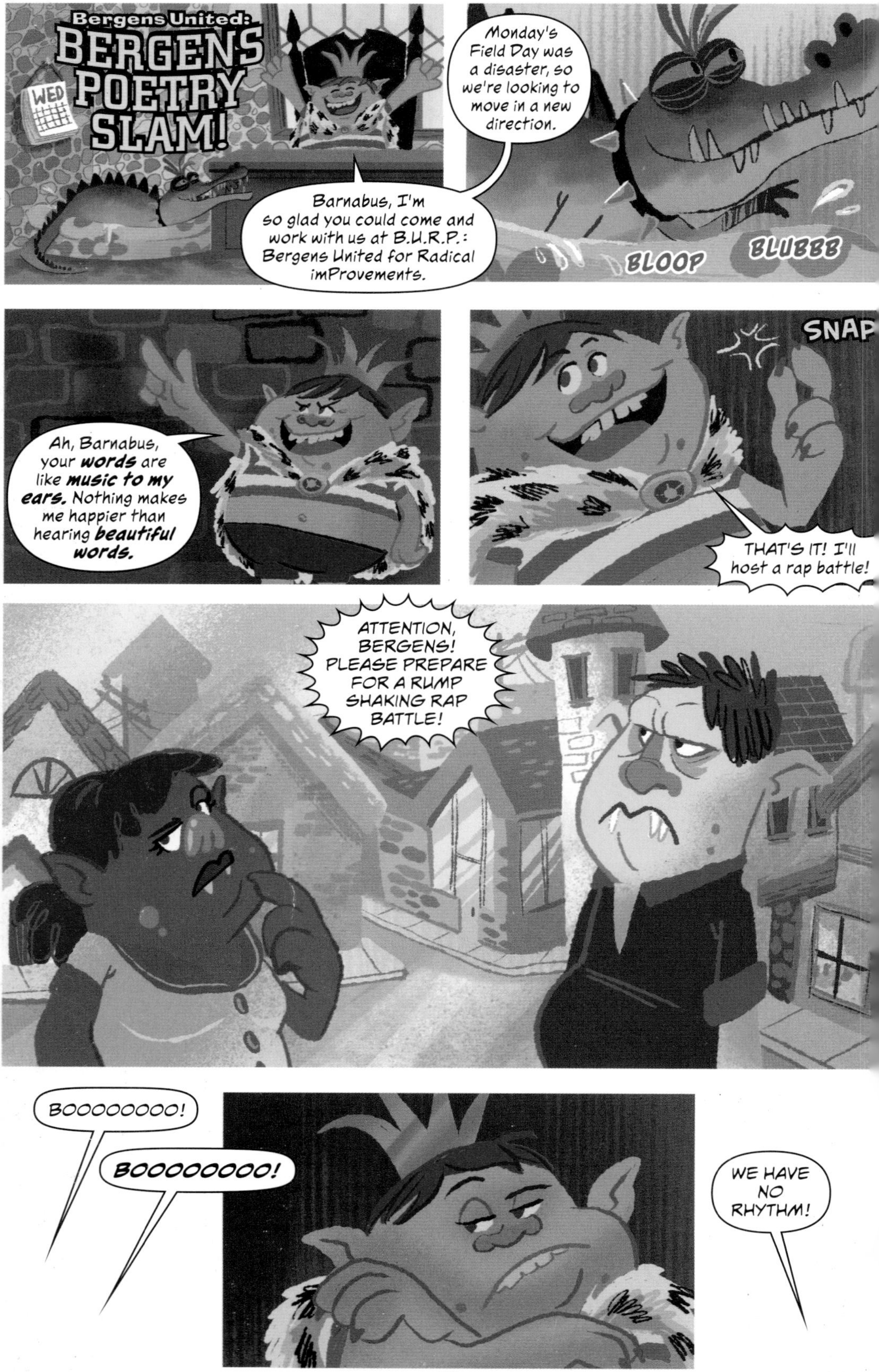
Bergens United: BERGENS POETRY SLAM!
WED
Barnabus, I'm so glad you could come and work with us at B.U.R.P.: Bergens United for Radical imProvements.
Monday's Field Day was a disaster, so we're looking to move in a new direction.
BLOOP
BLUBBB
Ah, Barnabus, your words are like music to my ears. Nothing makes me happier than hearing beautiful words.
SNAP
THAT'S IT! I'll host a rap battle!
ATTENTION, BERGENS! PLEASE PREPARE FOR A RUMP SHAKING RAP BATTLE!
BOOOOOOOO!
BOOOOOOOO!
WE HAVE NO RHYTHM!

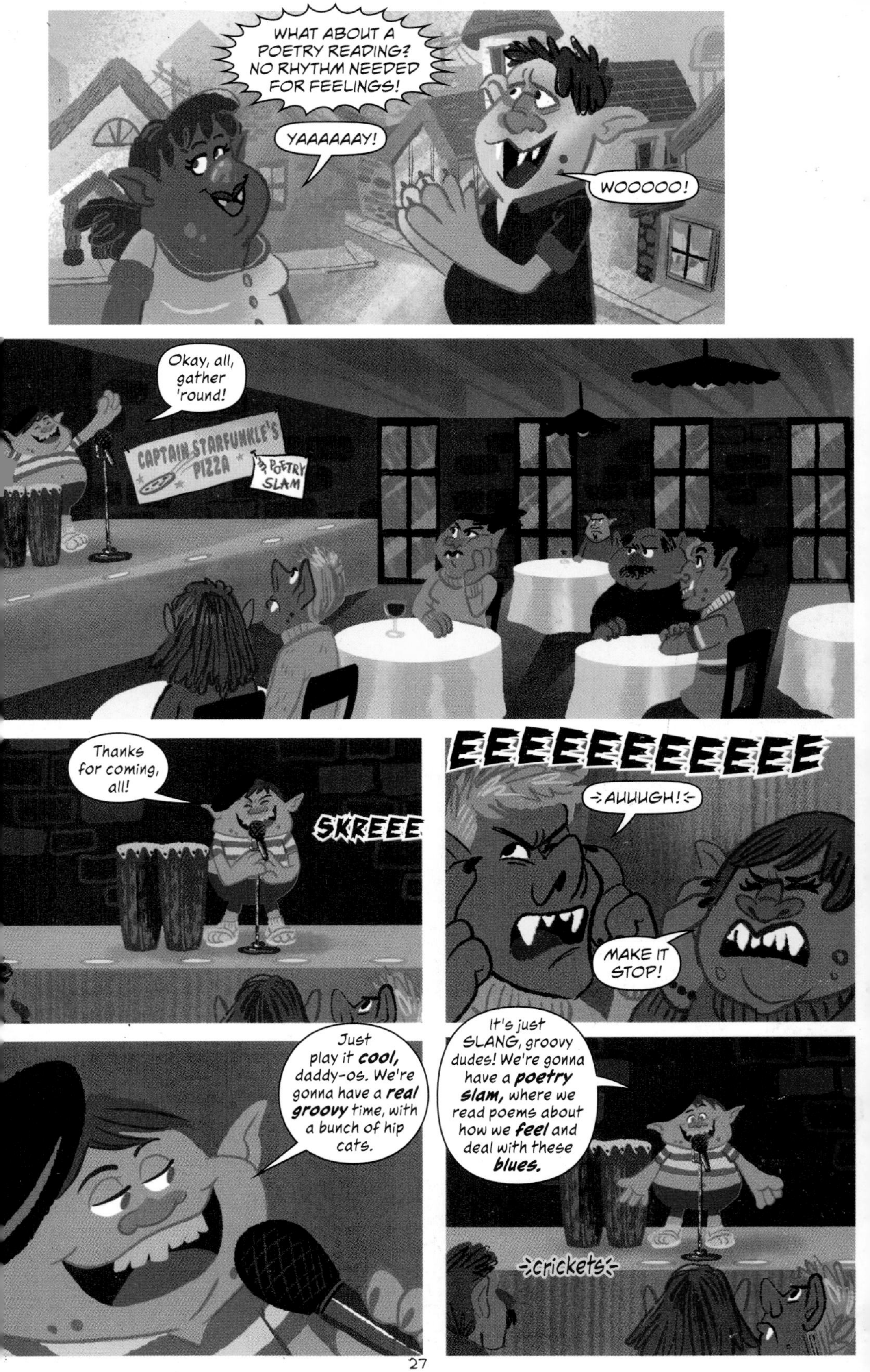
WHAT ABOUT A POETRY READING? NO RHYTHM NEEDED FOR FEELINGS!
YAAAAAAY!
WOOOOO!
Okay, all, gather 'round!
CAPTAIN STARFUNKLE'S PIZZA
POETRY SLAM
Thanks for coming, all!
SKREEE
EEEEEEEEEEEE
AUUUGH!
MAKE IT STOP!
Just play it **cool,** daddy-os. We're gonna have a **real groovy** time, with a bunch of hip cats.
It's just SLANG, groovy dudes! We're gonna have a **poetry slam,** where we read poems about how we **feel** and deal with these **blues.**
crickets

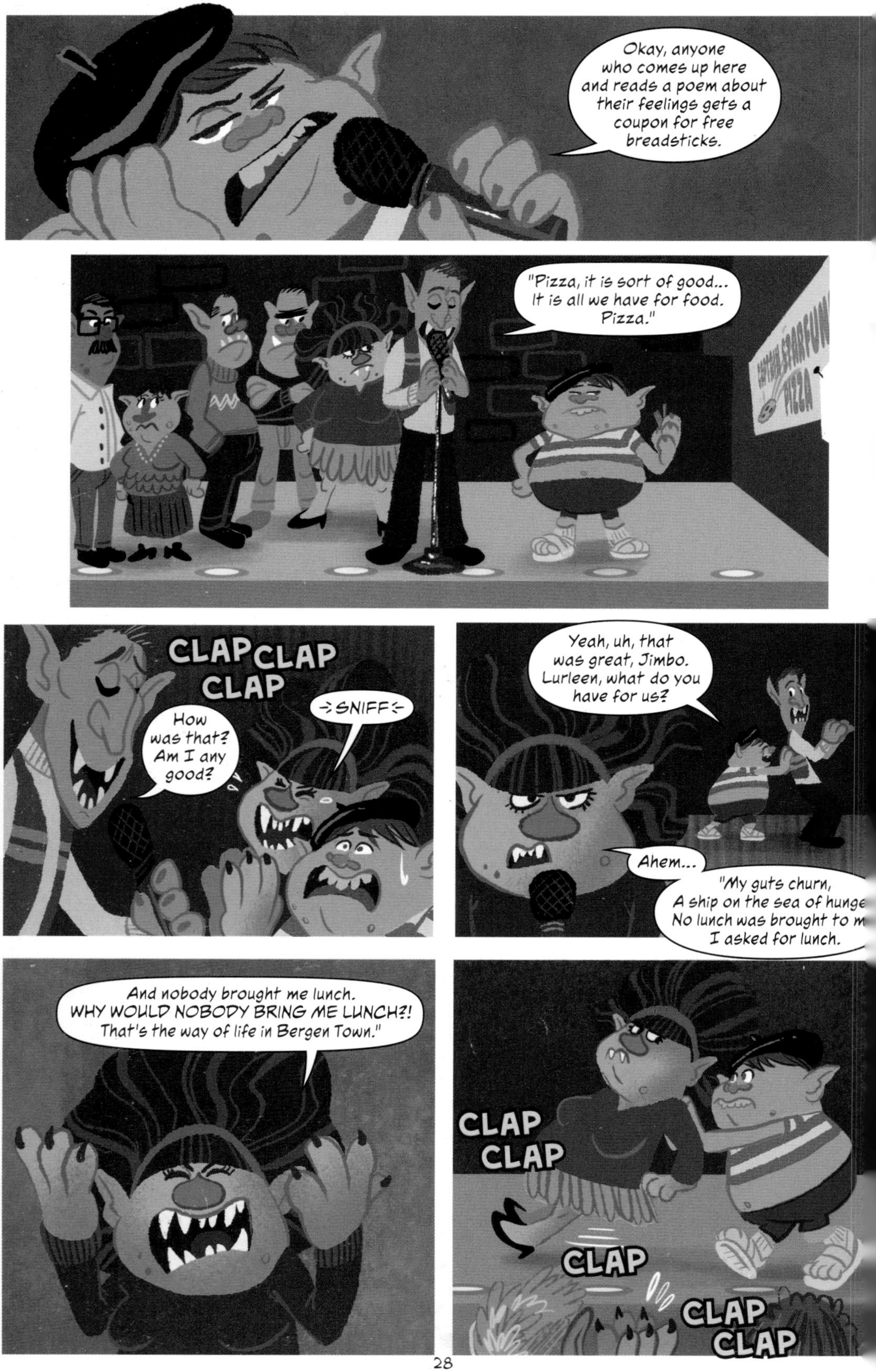

Okay, anyone who comes up here and reads a poem about their feelings gets a coupon for free breadsticks.
"Pizza, it is sort of good... It is all we have for food. Pizza."
CAPTAIN STARFUNKLE'S PIZZA
CLAP CLAP CLAP
How was that? Am I any good?
SNIFF
Yeah, uh, that was great, Jimbo. Lurleen, what do you have for us?
Ahem...
"My guts churn, A ship on the sea of hunge
No lunch was brought to m
I asked for lunch.
And nobody brought me lunch. WHY WOULD NOBODY BRING ME LUNCH?! That's the way of life in Bergen Town."
CLAP CLAP
CLAP
CLAP CLAP

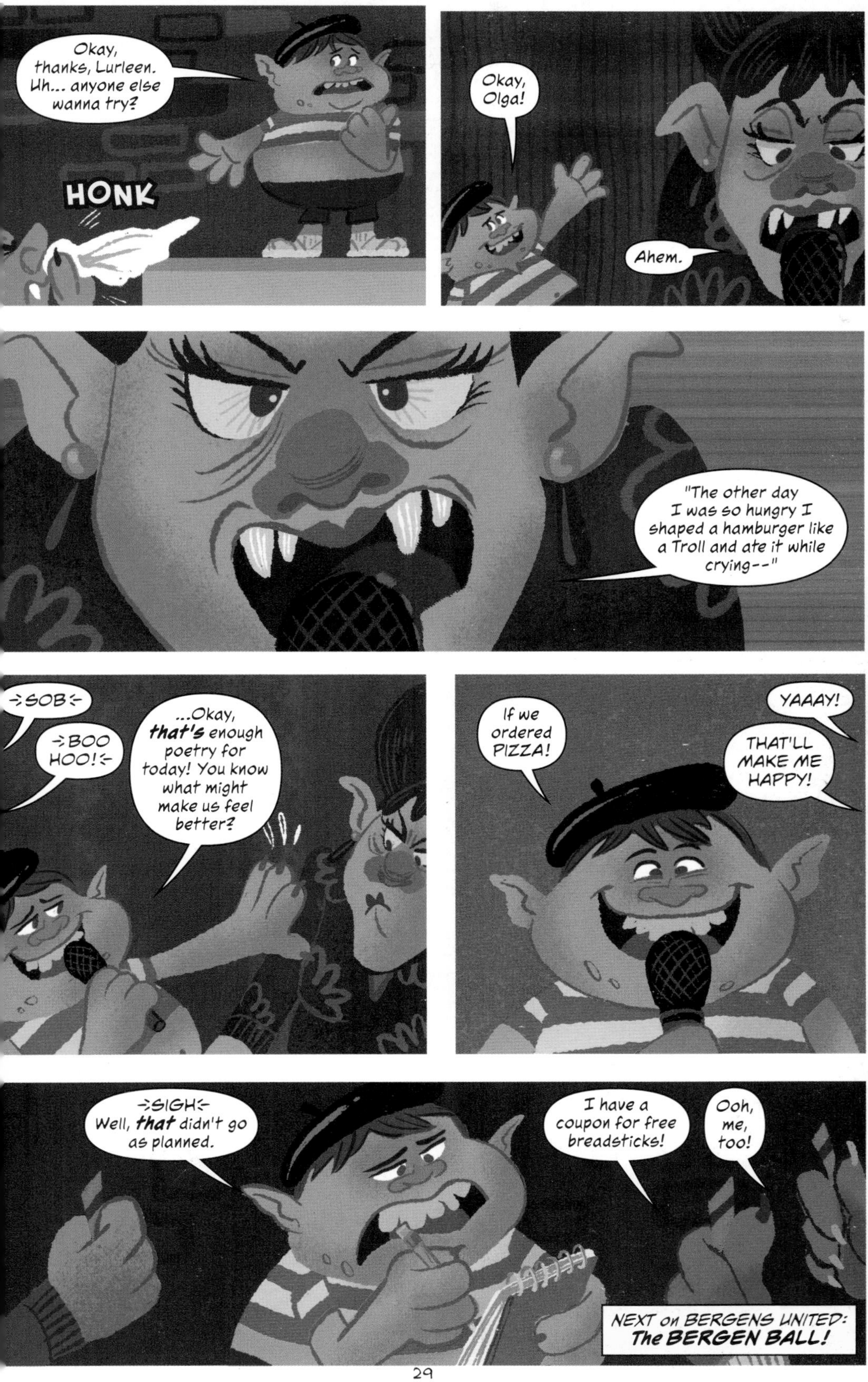
Okay, thanks, Lurleen. Uh... anyone else wanna try?
HONK
Okay, Olga!
Ahem.
"The other day I was so hungry I shaped a hamburger like a Troll and ate it while crying--"
SOB
BOO HOO!
...Okay, that's enough poetry for today! You know what might make us feel better?
If we ordered PIZZA!
YAAAY!
THAT'LL MAKE ME HAPPY!
SIGH Well, that didn't go as planned.
I have a coupon for free breadsticks!
Ooh, me, too!
NEXT on BERGENS UNITED: The BERGEN BALL!

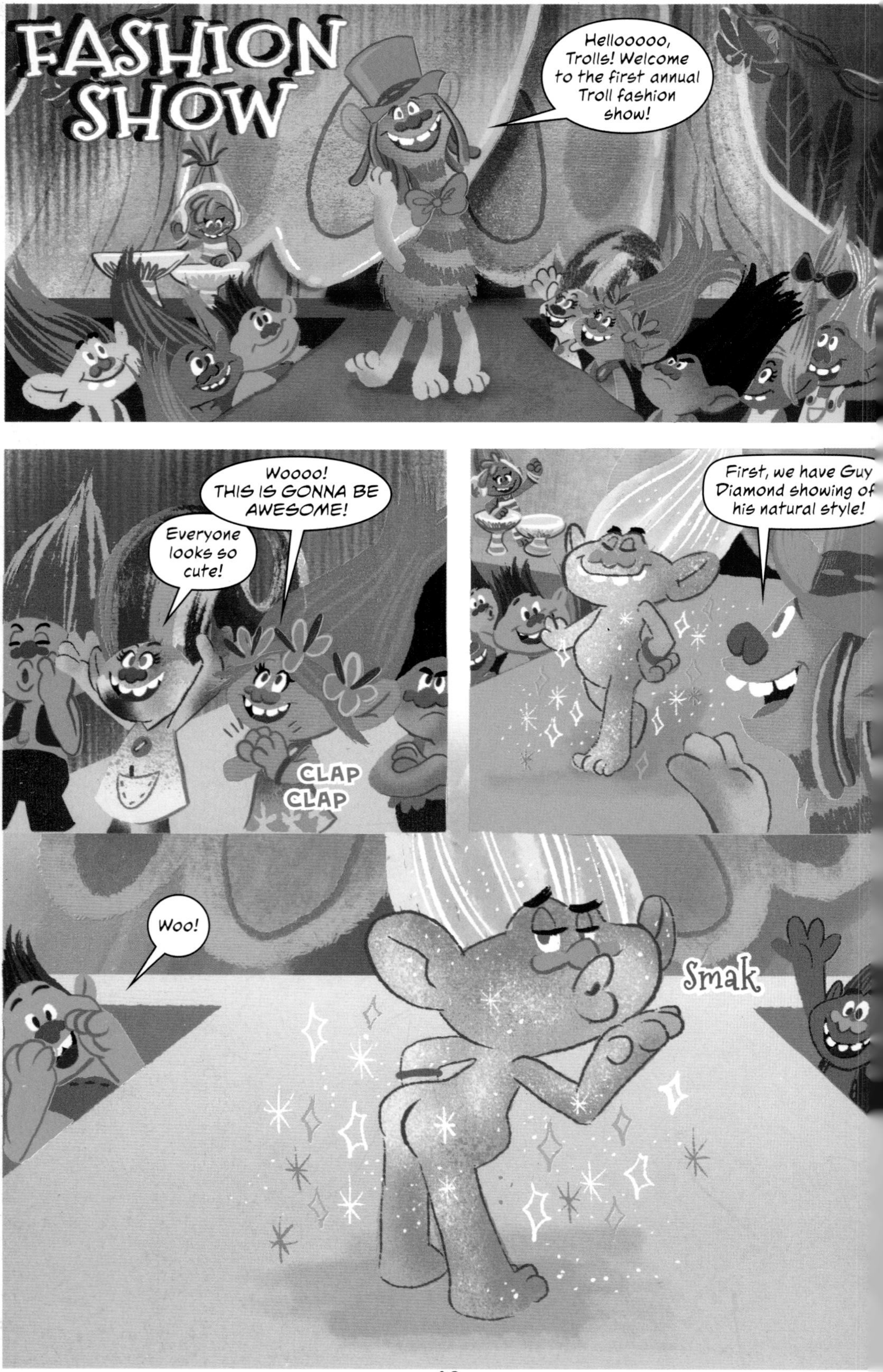
FASHION SHOW
Hellooooo, Trolls! Welcome to the first annual Troll fashion show!
Everyone looks so cute!
Woooo! THIS IS GONNA BE AWESOME!
CLAP CLAP
First, we have Guy Diamond showing of his natural style!
Woo!
Smak

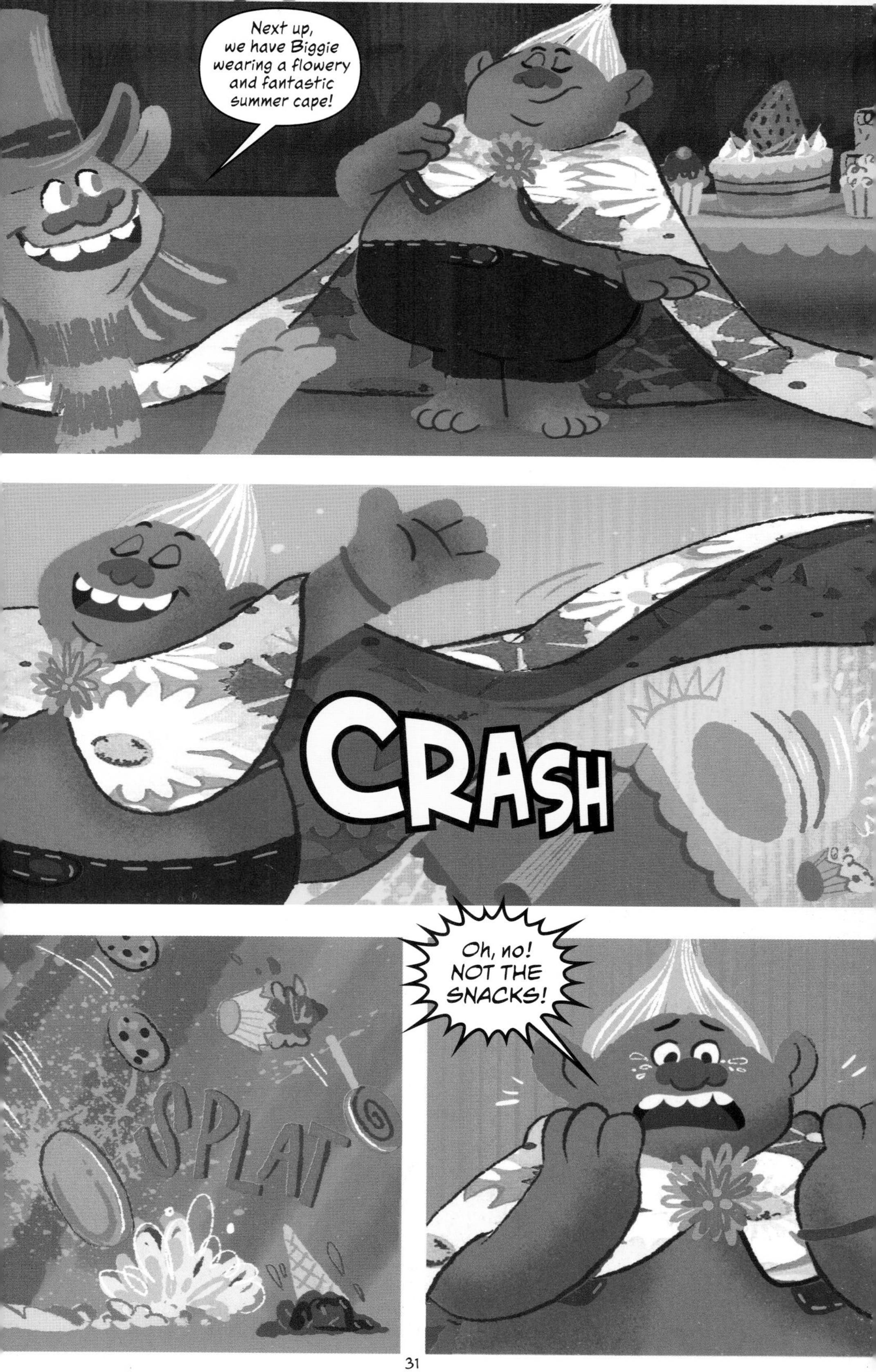
Next up, we have Biggie wearing a flowery and fantastic summer cape!
CRASH
SPLAT
Oh, no! NOT THE SNACKS!

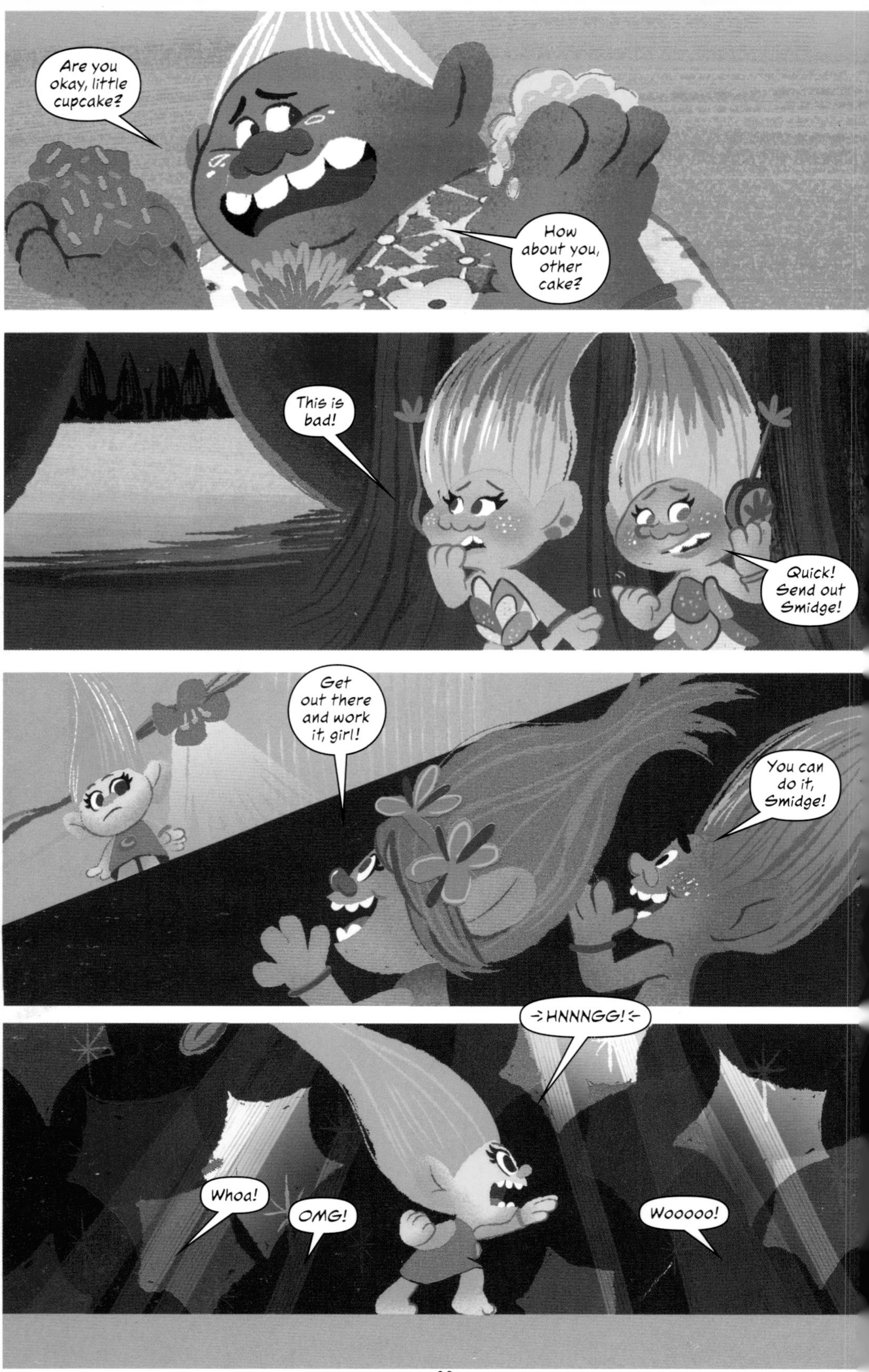
Are you okay, little cupcake?
How about you, other cake?
This is bad!
Quick! Send out Smidge!
Get out there and work it, girl!
You can do it, Smidge!
HNNNGG!
Whoa!
OMG!
Wooooo!

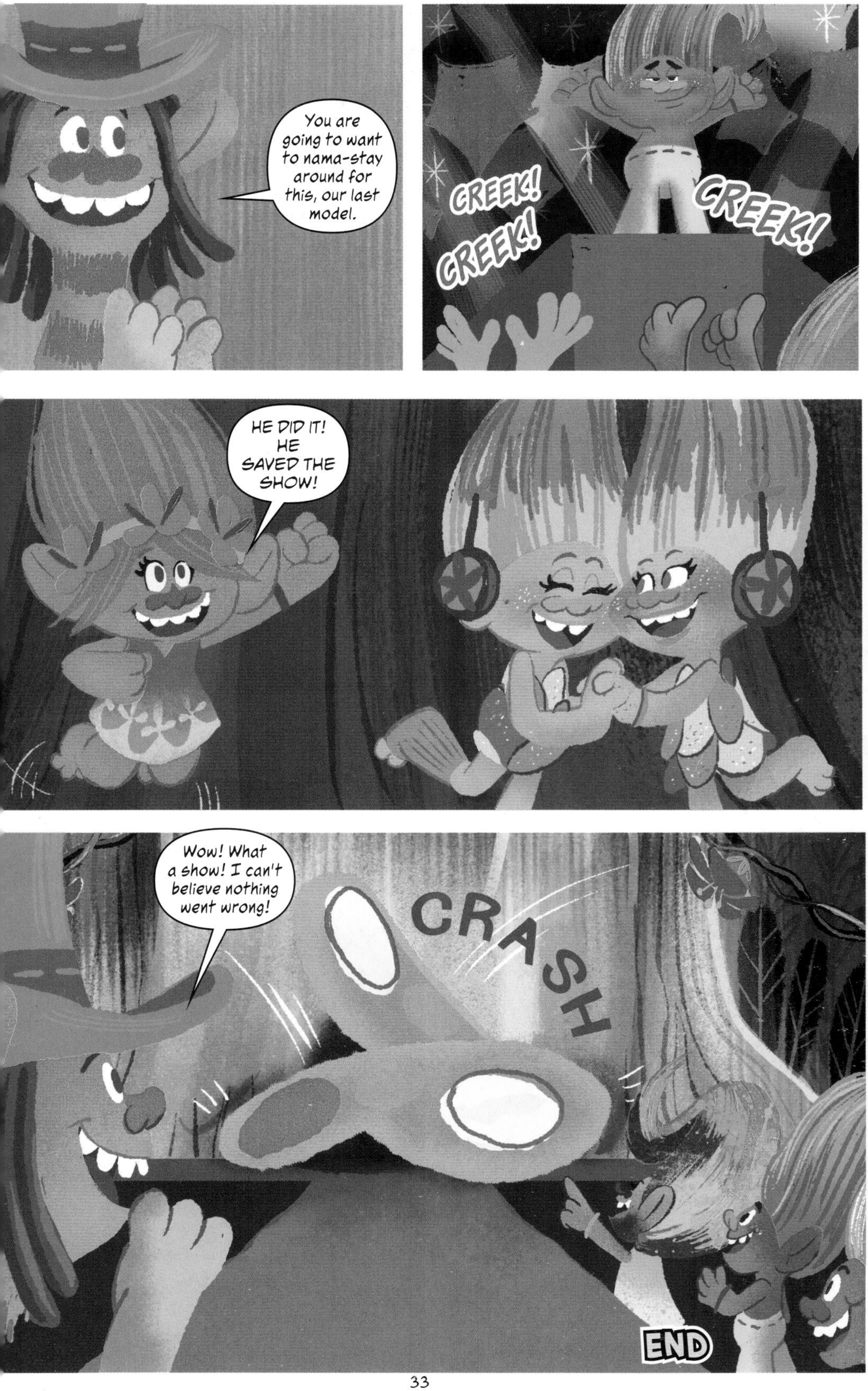

You are going to want to nama-stay around for this, our last model.
CREEK!
CREEK!
CREEK!
HE DID IT! HE SAVED THE SHOW!
Wow! What a show! I can't believe nothing went wrong!
CRASH
END

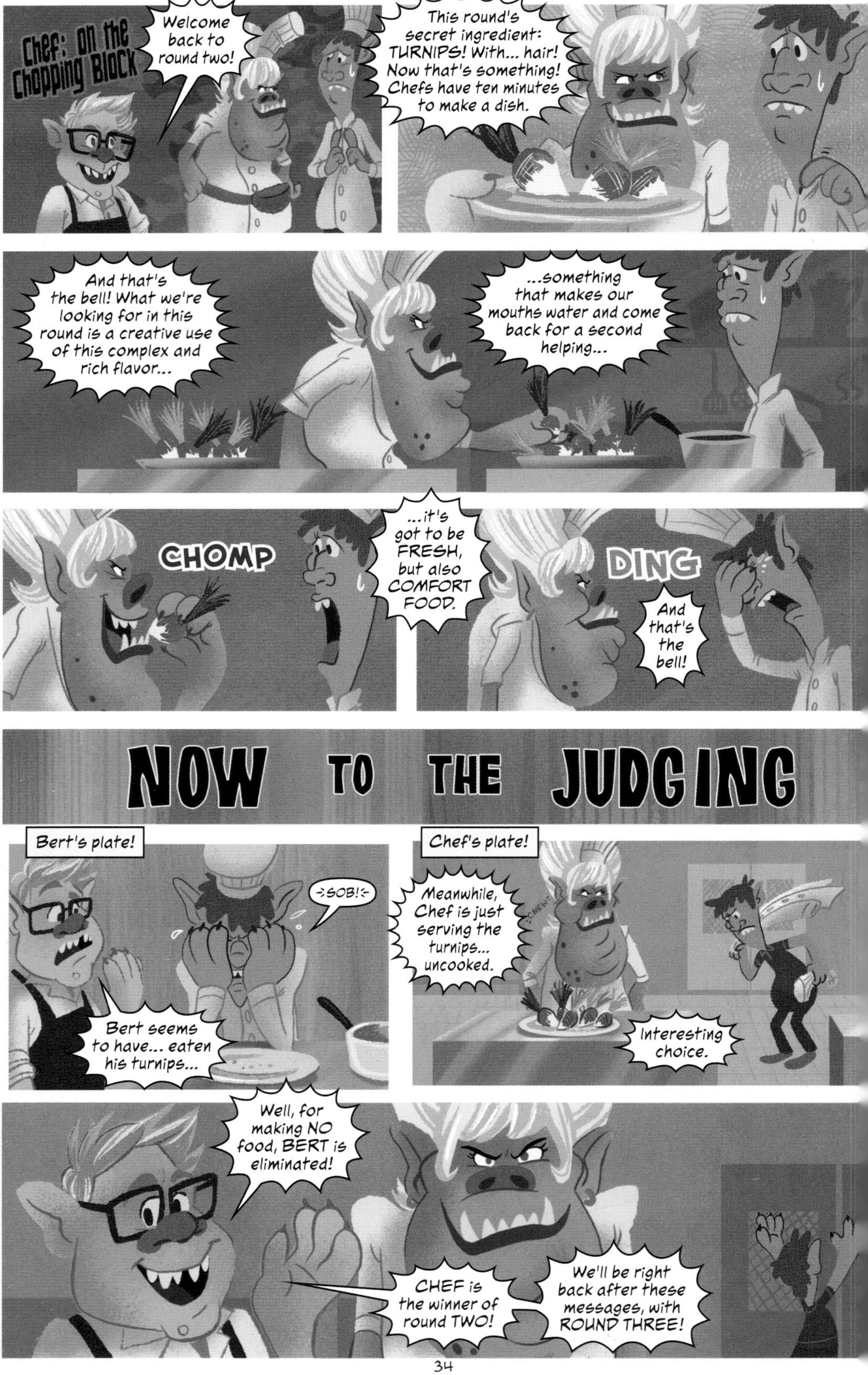
Chef: on the Chopping Block
Welcome back to round two!
This round's secret ingredient: TURNIPS! With... hair! Now that's something! Chefs have ten minutes to make a dish.
And that's the bell! What we're looking for in this round is a creative use of this complex and rich flavor...
...something that makes our mouths water and come back for a second helping...
CHOMP
...it's got to be FRESH, but also COMFORT FOOD.
DING
And that's the bell!
NOW TO THE JUDGING
Bert's plate!
-SOB!-
Bert seems to have... eaten his turnips...
Chef's plate!
Meanwhile, Chef is just serving the turnips... uncooked.
Interesting choice.
Well, for making NO food, BERT is eliminated!
CHEF is the winner of round TWO!
We'll be right back after these messages, with ROUND THREE!

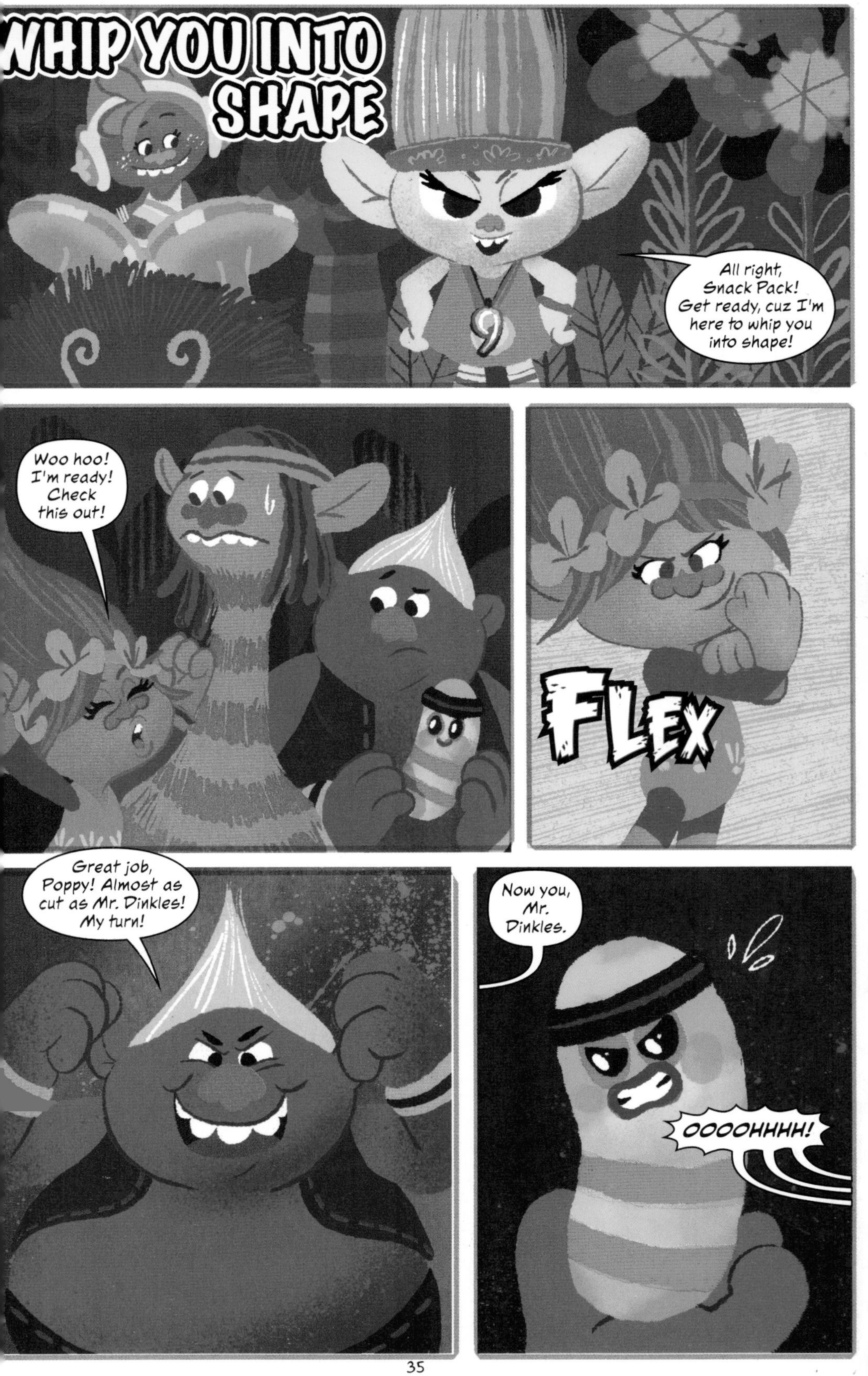
WHIP YOU INTO SHAPE
All right, Snack Pack! Get ready, cuz I'm here to whip you into shape!
Woo hoo! I'm ready! Check this out!
FLEX
Great job, Poppy! Almost as cut as Mr. Dinkles! My turn!
Now you, Mr. Dinkles.
OOOOHHHH!

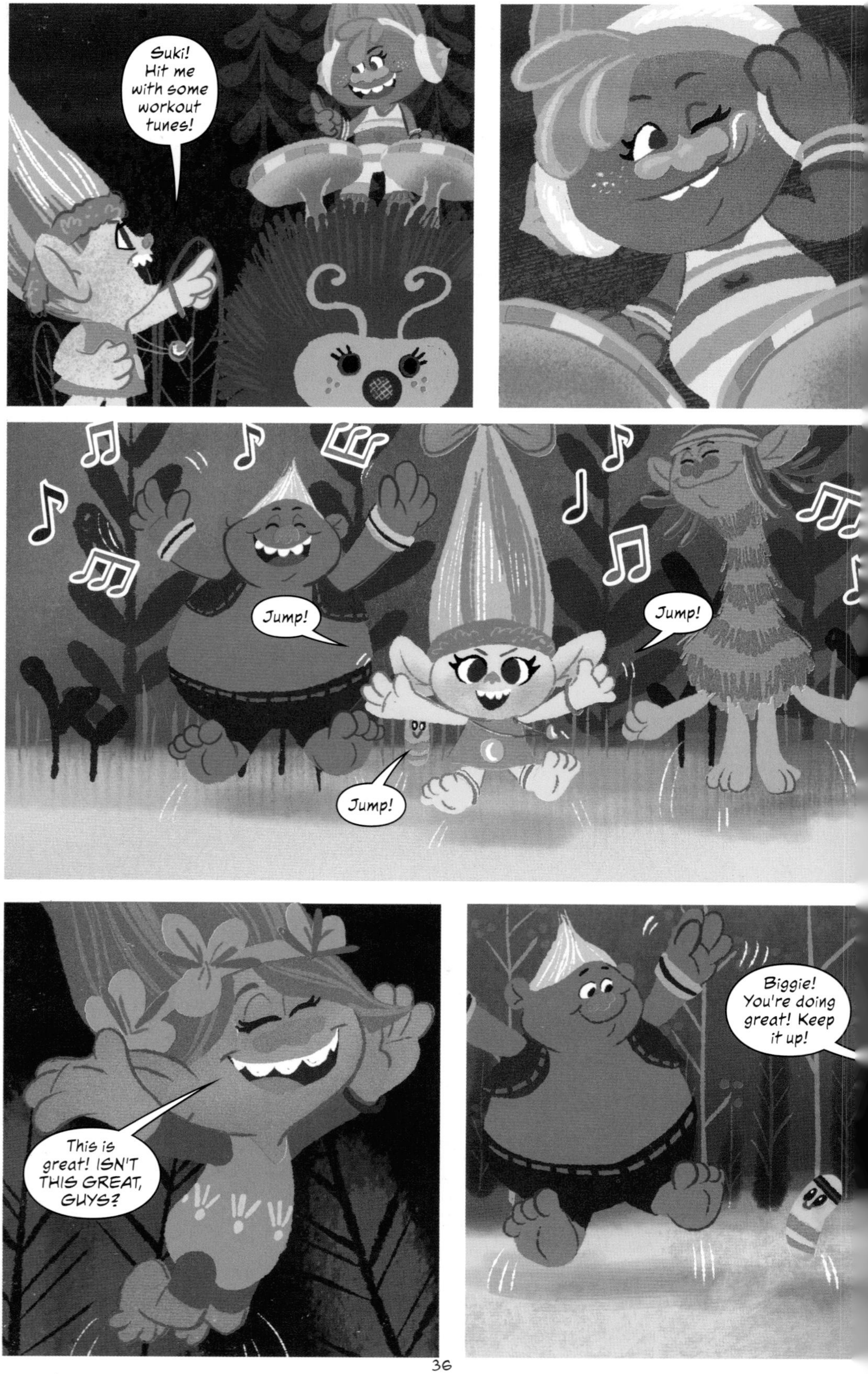

Suki! Hit me with some workout tunes!
Jump!
Jump!
Jump!
This is great! ISN'T THIS GREAT, GUYS?
Biggie! You're doing great! Keep it up!

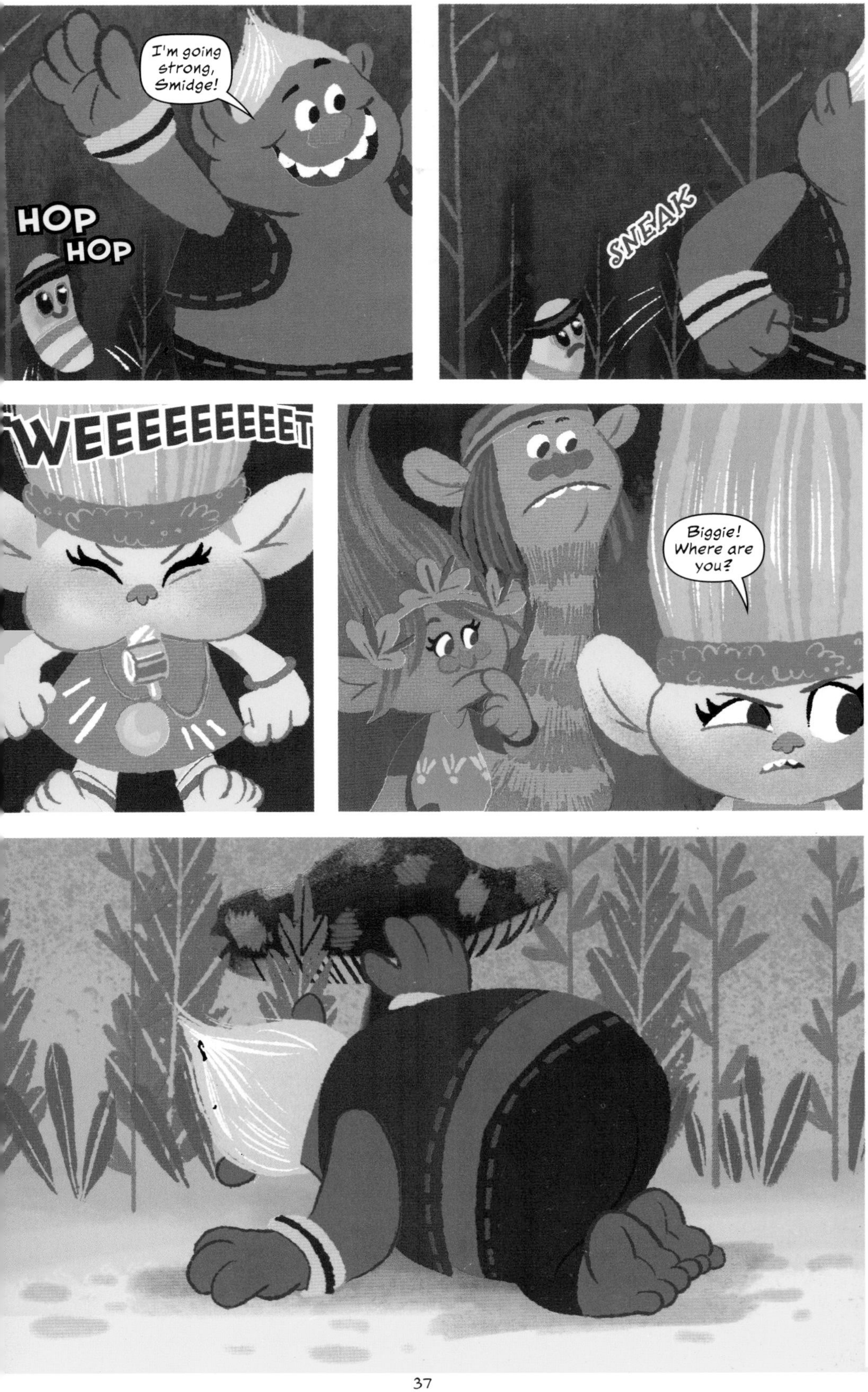
I'm going strong, Smidge!
HOP HOP
SNEAK
WEEEEEEEEET
Biggie! Where are you?

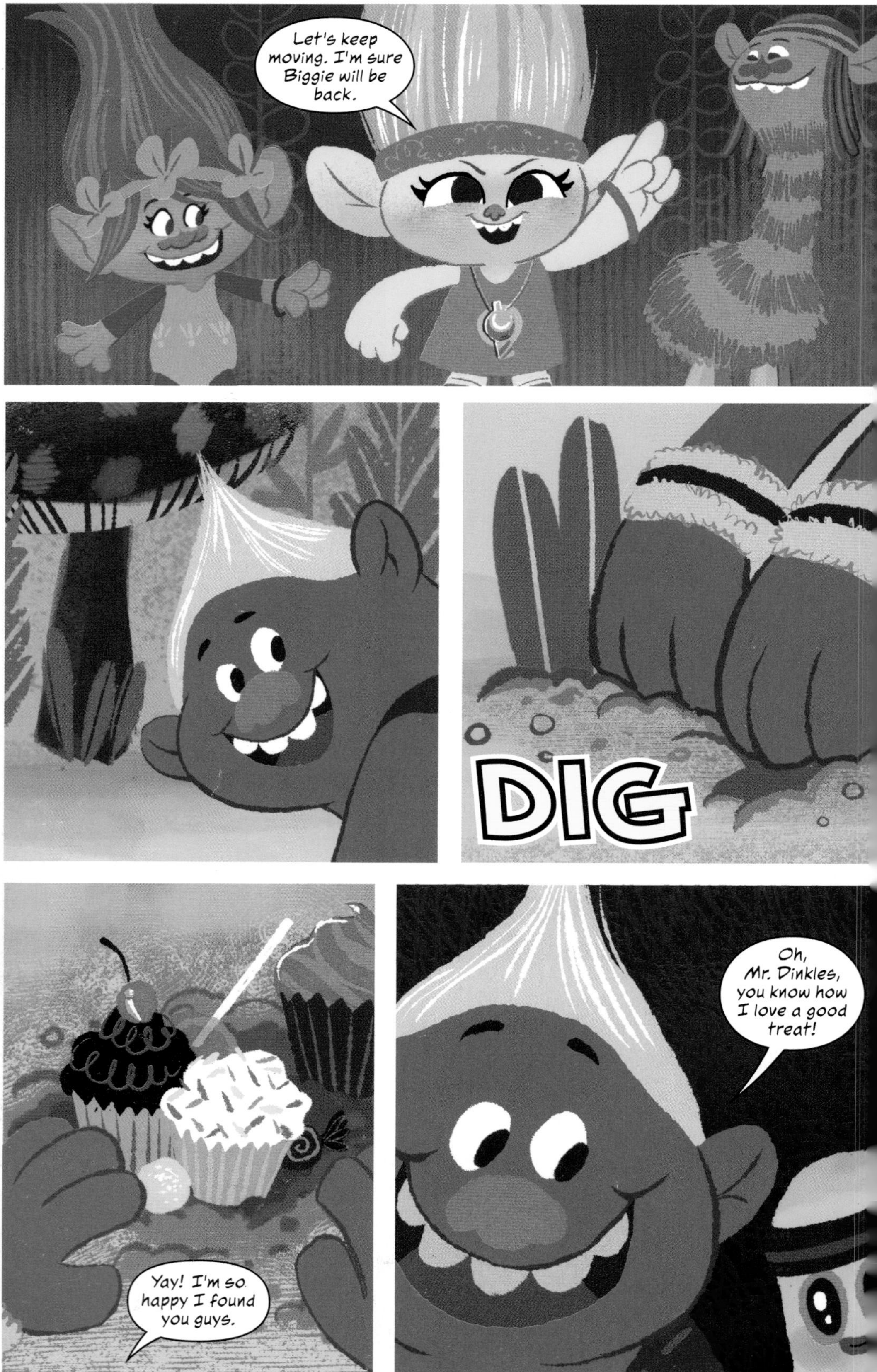
Let's keep moving. I'm sure Biggie will be back.
DIG
Yay! I'm so happy I found you guys.
Oh, Mr. Dinkles, you know how I love a good treat!

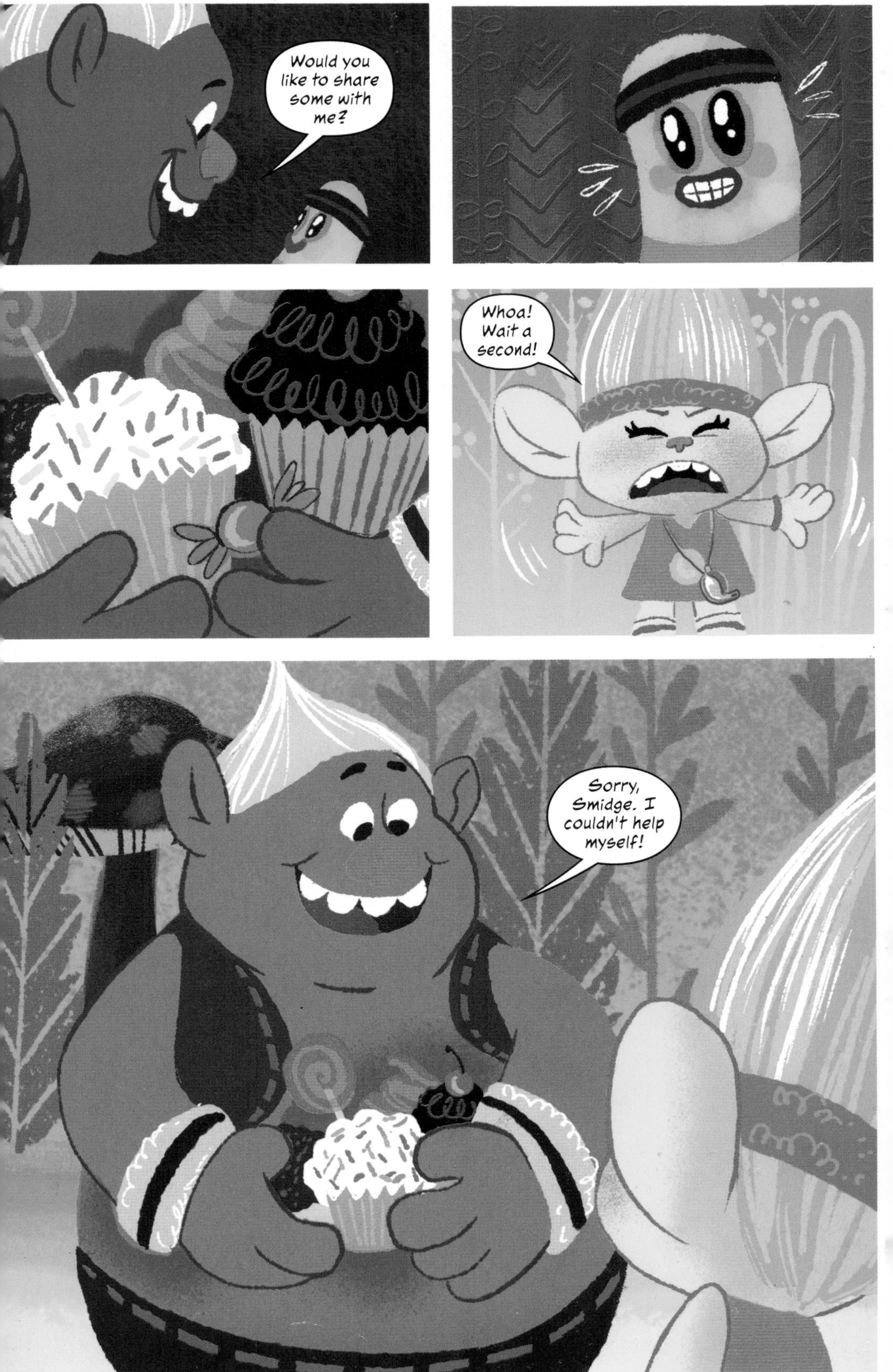
Would you like to share some with me?
Whoa! Wait a second!
Sorry, Smidge. I couldn't help myself!

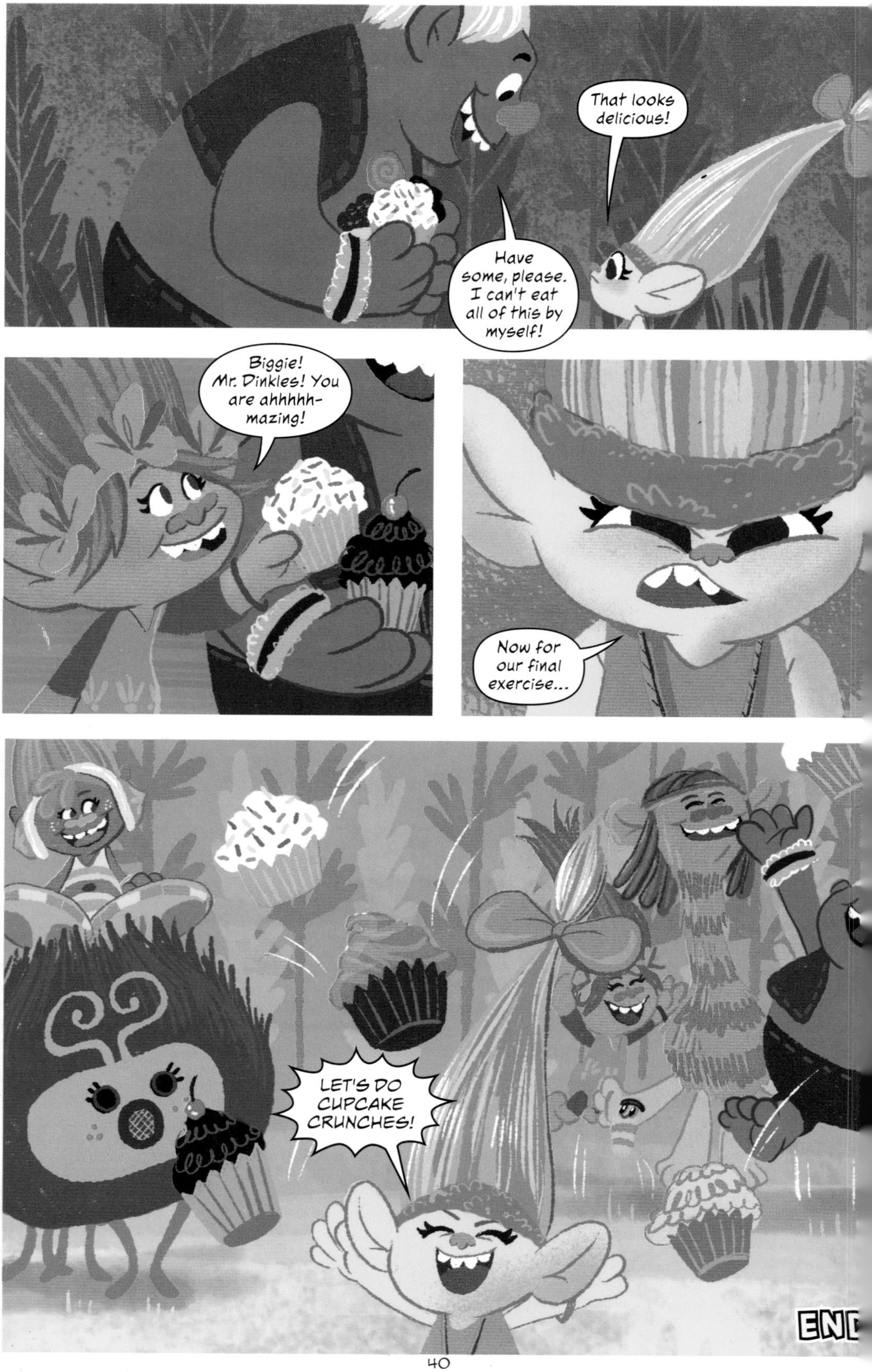
That looks delicious!
Have some, please. I can't eat all of this by myself!
Biggie! Mr. Dinkles! You are ahhhhh-mazing!
Now for our final exercise...
LET'S DO CUPCAKE CRUNCHES!
END

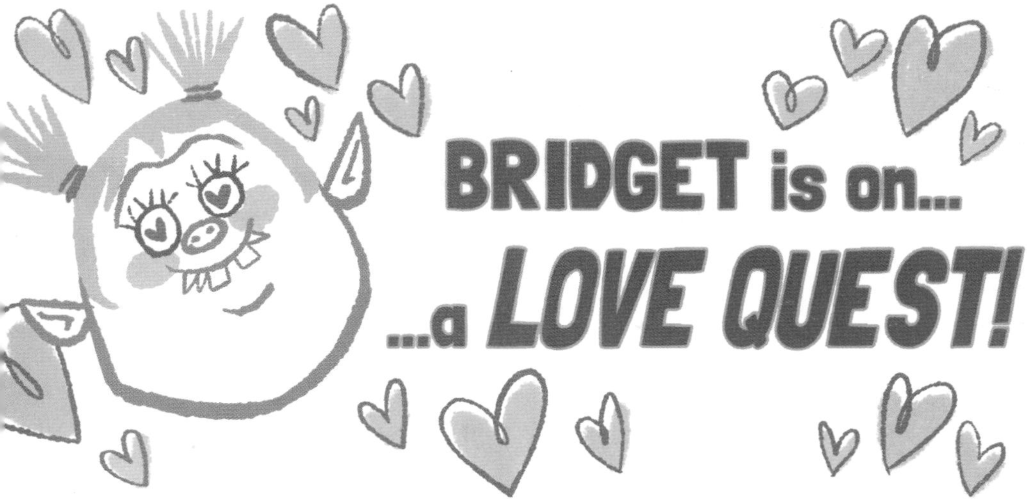
BRIDGET is on...
...a LOVE QUEST!

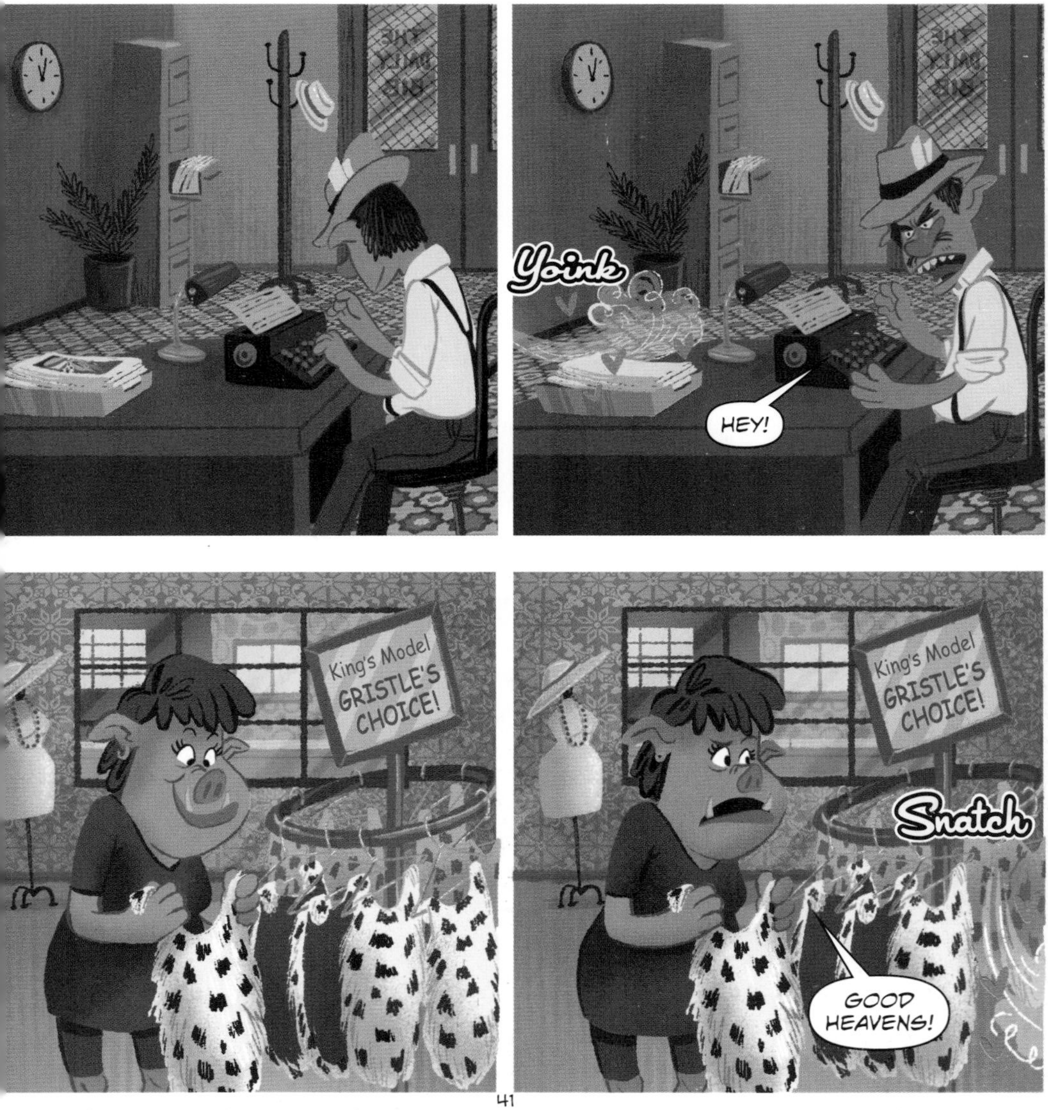
Yoink
HEY!
King's Model GRISTLE'S CHOICE!
King's Model GRISTLE'S CHOICE!
Snatch
GOOD HEAVENS!

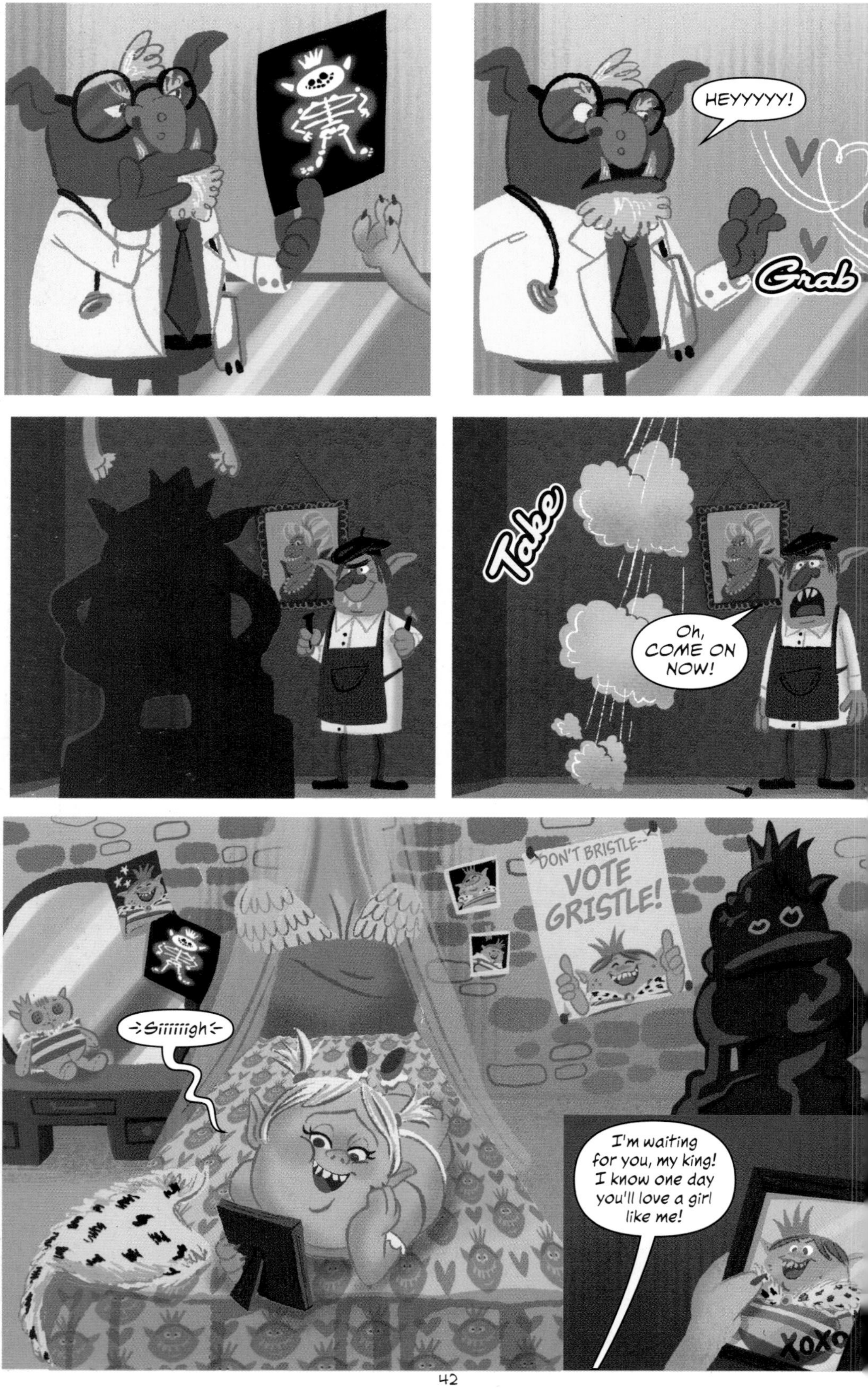
HEYYYYY!
Grab
Take
Oh, COME ON NOW!
DON'T BRISTLE-- VOTE GRISTLE!
~Siiiiiigh~
I'm waiting for you, my king! I know one day you'll love a girl like me!
XOXO

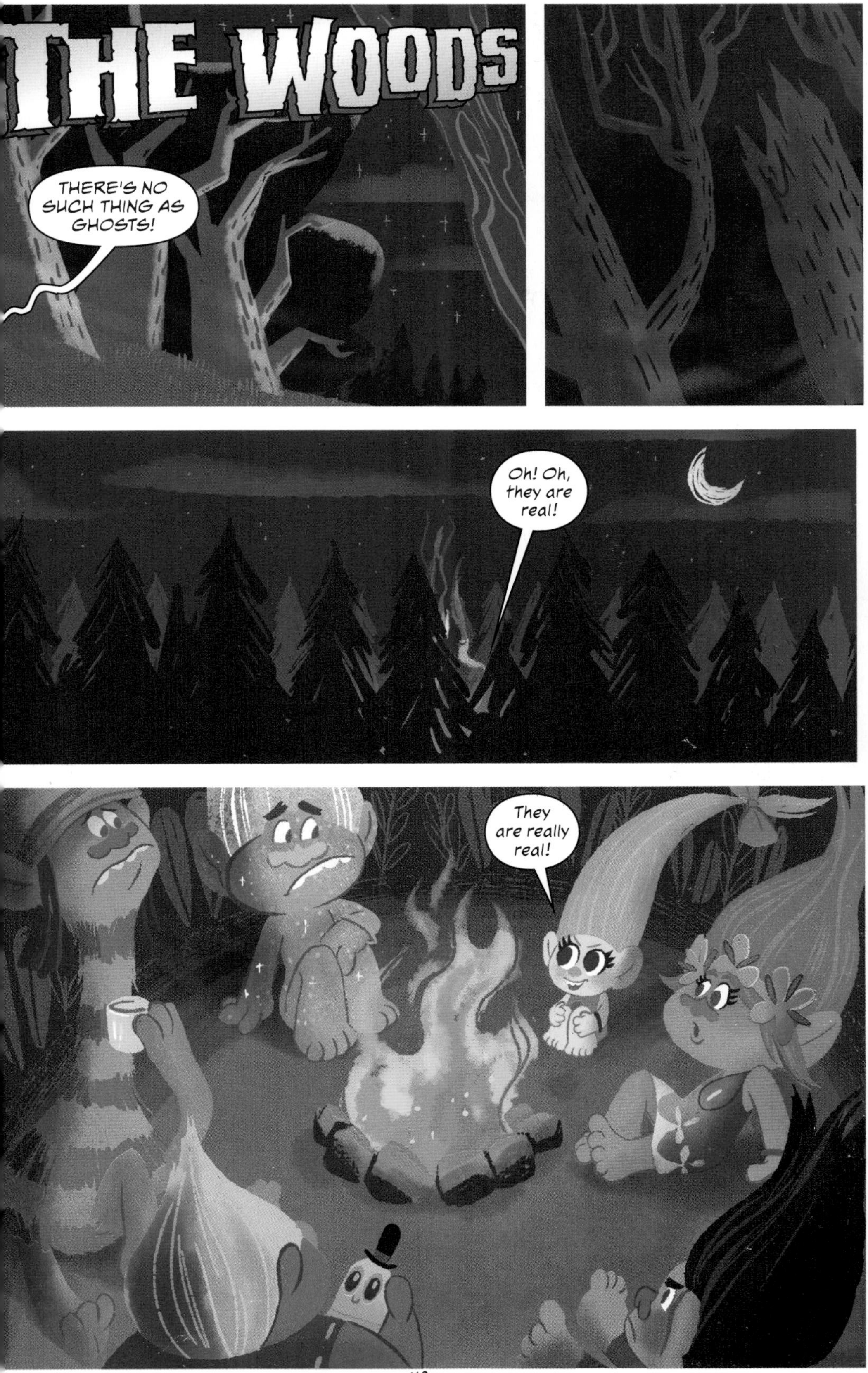
THE WOODS
THERE'S NO SUCH THING AS GHOSTS!
Oh! Oh, they are real!
They are really real!

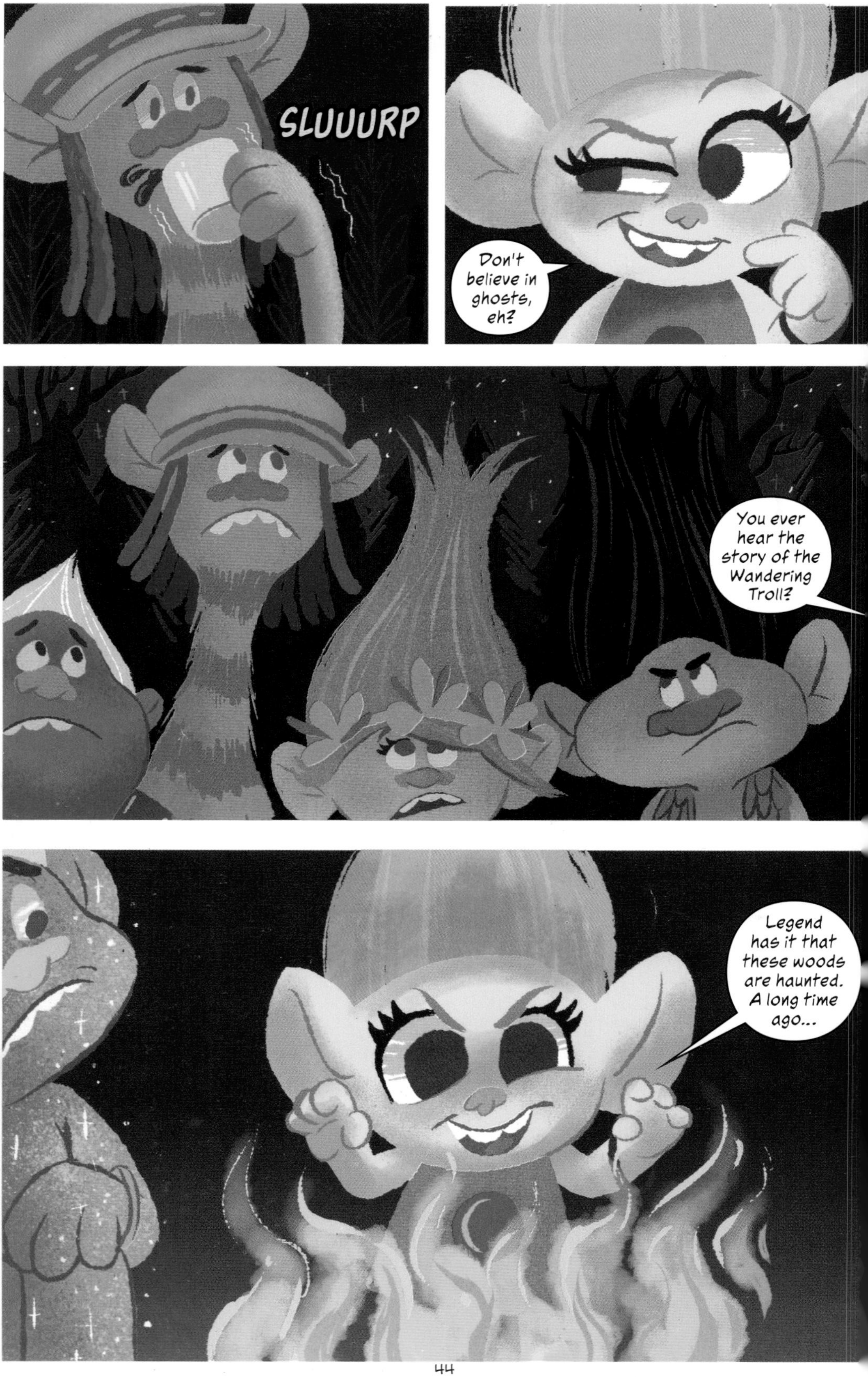

SLUUURP
Don't believe in ghosts, eh?
You ever hear the story of the Wandering Troll?
Legend has it that these woods are haunted. A long time ago...

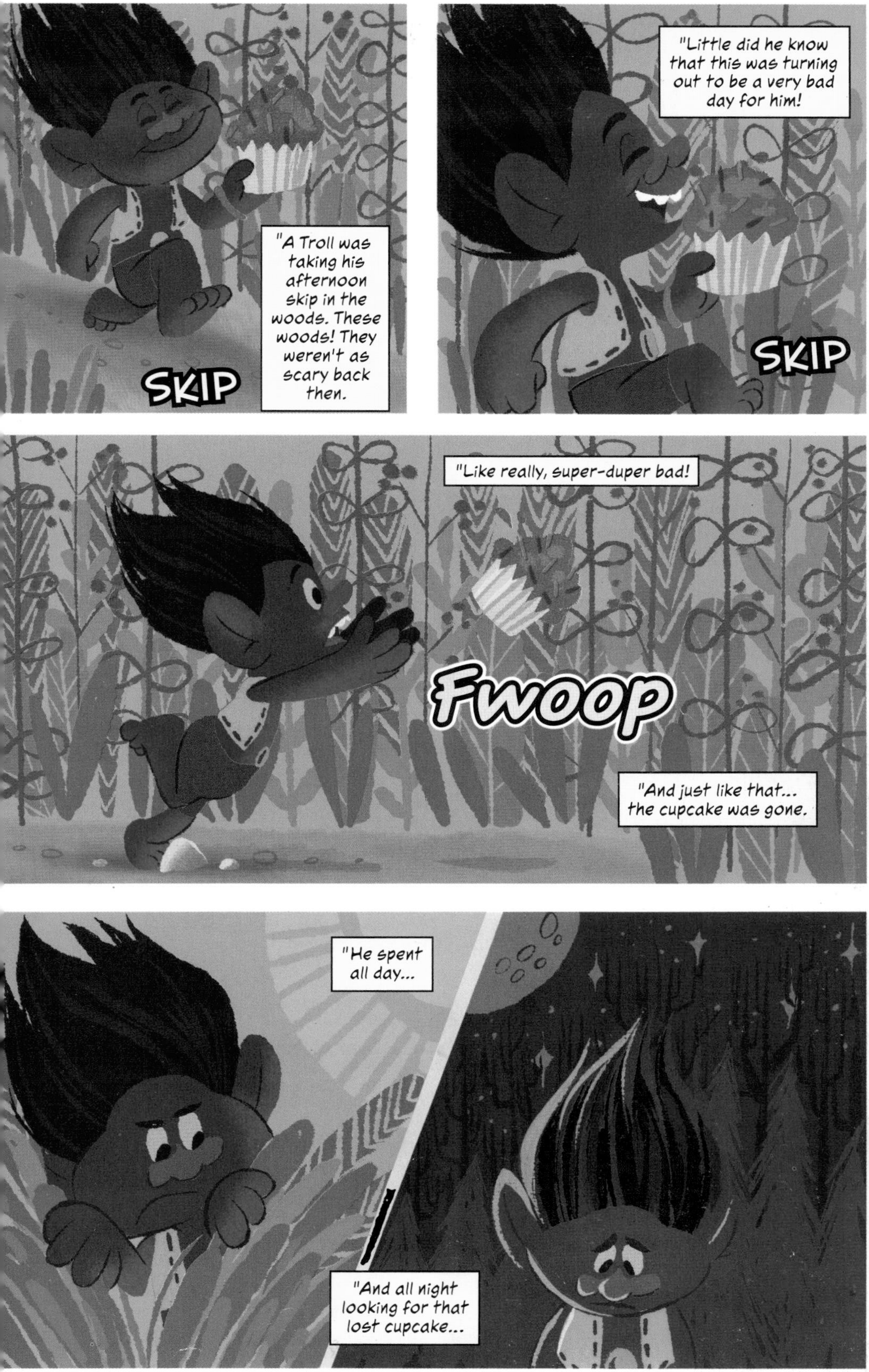
"A Troll was taking his afternoon skip in the woods. These woods! They weren't as scary back then.
SKIP
"Little did he know that this was turning out to be a very bad day for him!
SKIP
"Like really, super-duper bad!
Fwoop
"And just like that... the cupcake was gone.
"He spent all day...
"And all night looking for that lost cupcake...

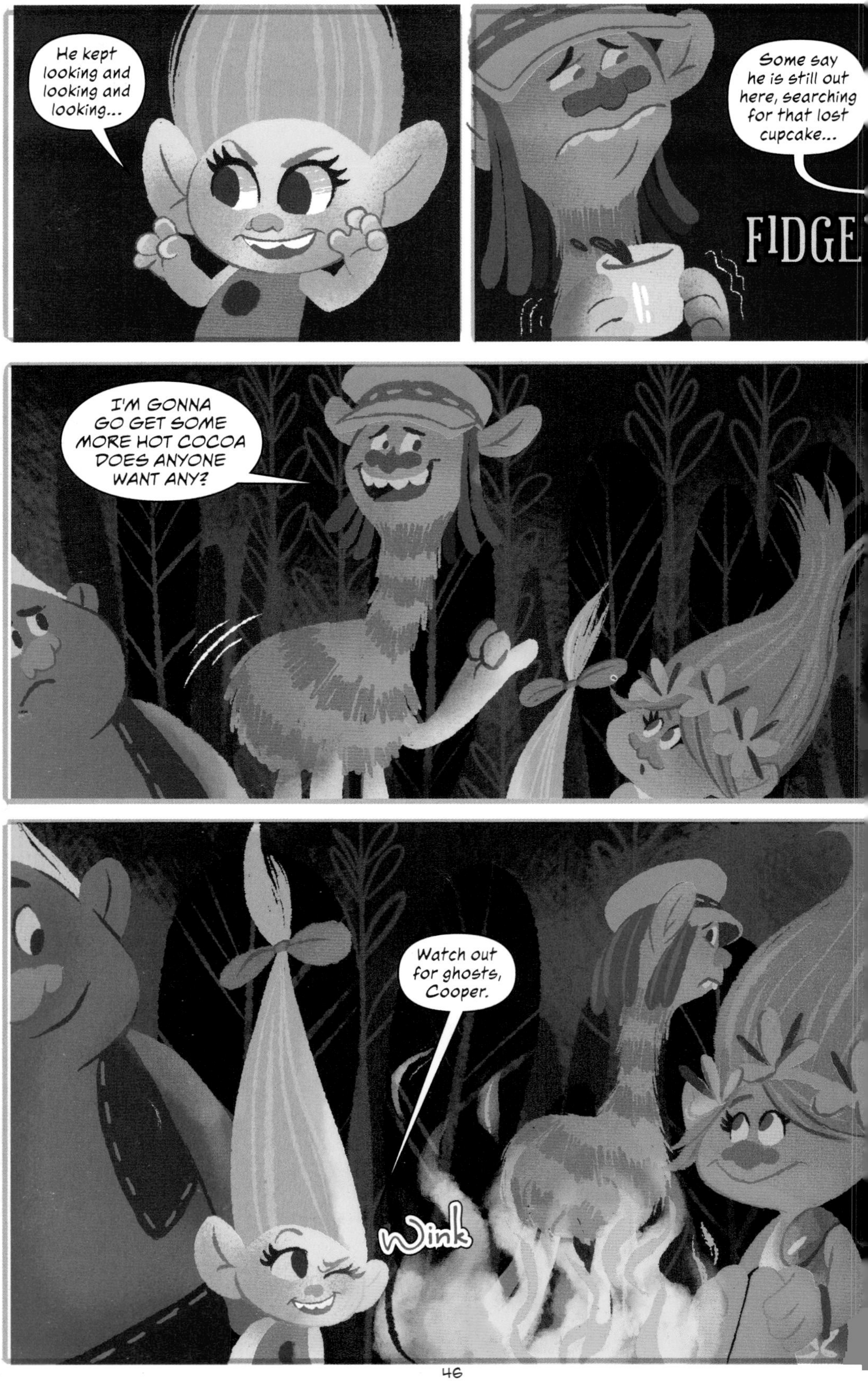
He kept looking and looking and looking...
Some say he is still out here, searching for that lost cupcake...
FIDGE
I'M GONNA GO GET SOME MORE HOT COCOA DOES ANYONE WANT ANY?
Watch out for ghosts, Cooper.
Wink

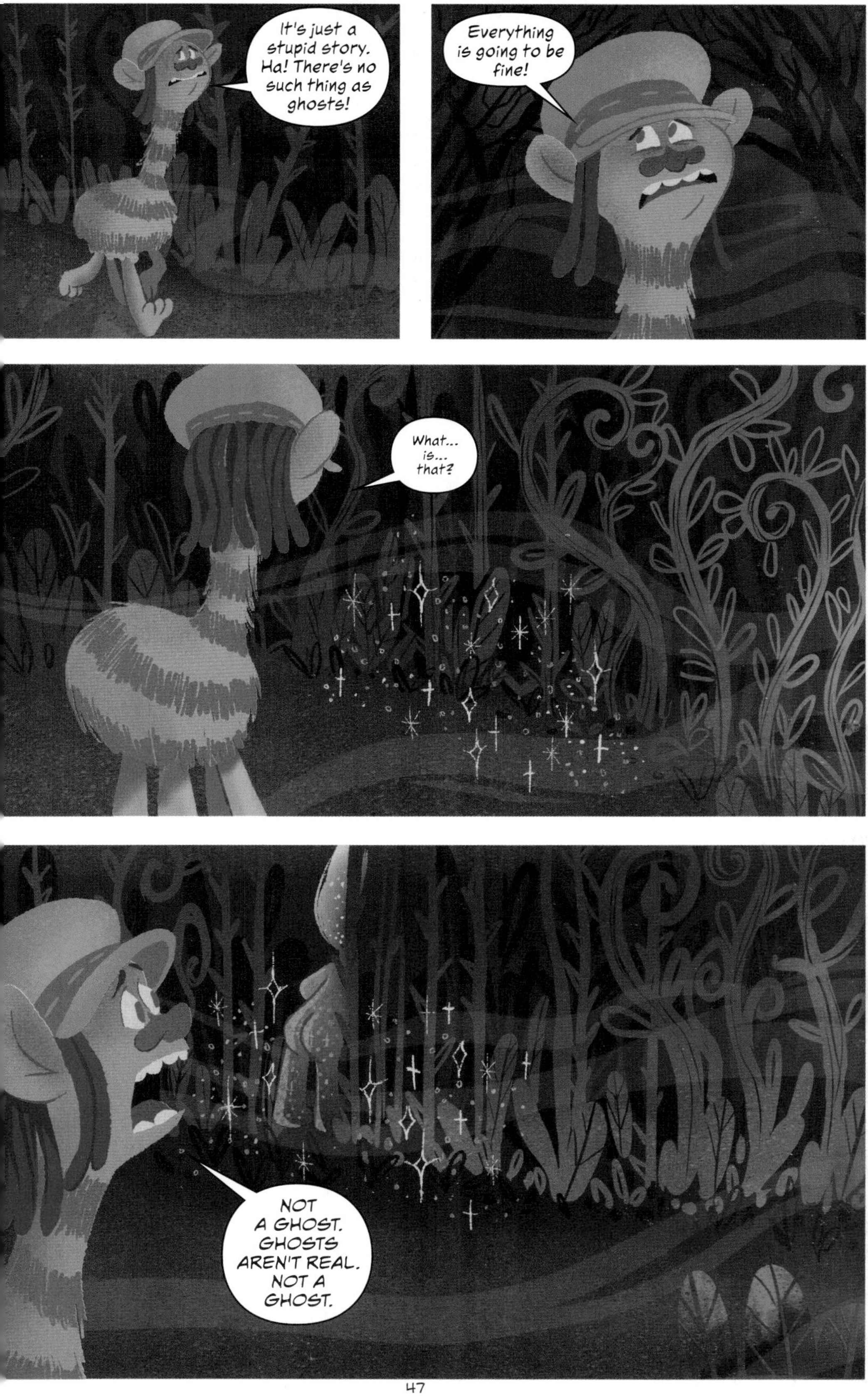
It's just a stupid story. Ha! There's no such thing as ghosts!
Everything is going to be fine!
What... is... that?
NOT A GHOST. GHOSTS AREN'T REAL. NOT A GHOST.

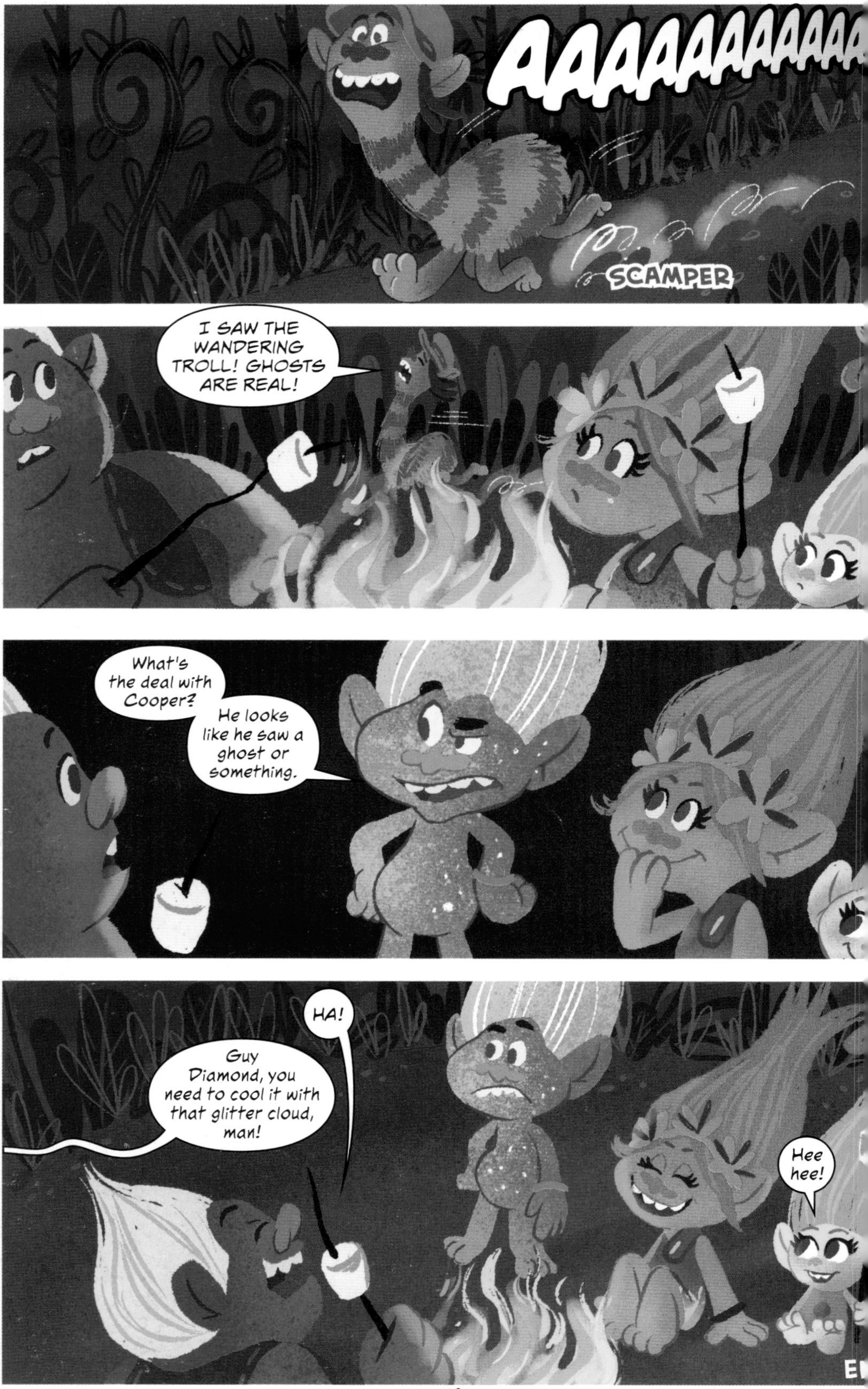
AAAAAAAAAAA
SCAMPER
I SAW THE WANDERING TROLL! GHOSTS ARE REAL!
What's the deal with Cooper?
He looks like he saw a ghost or something.
HA!
Guy Diamond, you need to cool it with that glitter cloud, man!
Hee hee!

w time for the FINAL ROUND of...

CHEFS ON THE OPPING BLOCK!

CHEF

This round, our final chef simply has to create a recipe with our secret ingredient...

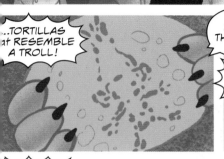

...TORTILLAS at RESEMBLE A TROLL!

TROLL TORTILLAS? I went through this WHOLE THING because I was told there would be REAL TROLLS.

Sorry, that isn't possible.

ut it really does ok like a Troll on ere, doesn't it?

SMASH

WHAM
WHAM
WHAM
WHAM
WHAM
WHAM

WHY ARE WE EVEN WASTING OUR TIME IF WE CAN'T HAVE REAL TROLLS?

I WAS PROMISED RARE AND DELICIOUS TROLLS!

And it appears CHEF has made... angry tortilla mush. Great! That's our show--

Oh, no. Keep her out of the REFRIGERATOR!

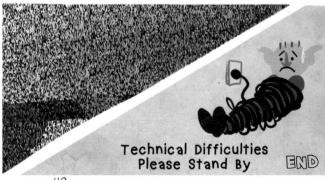

Technical Difficulties
Please Stand By

END

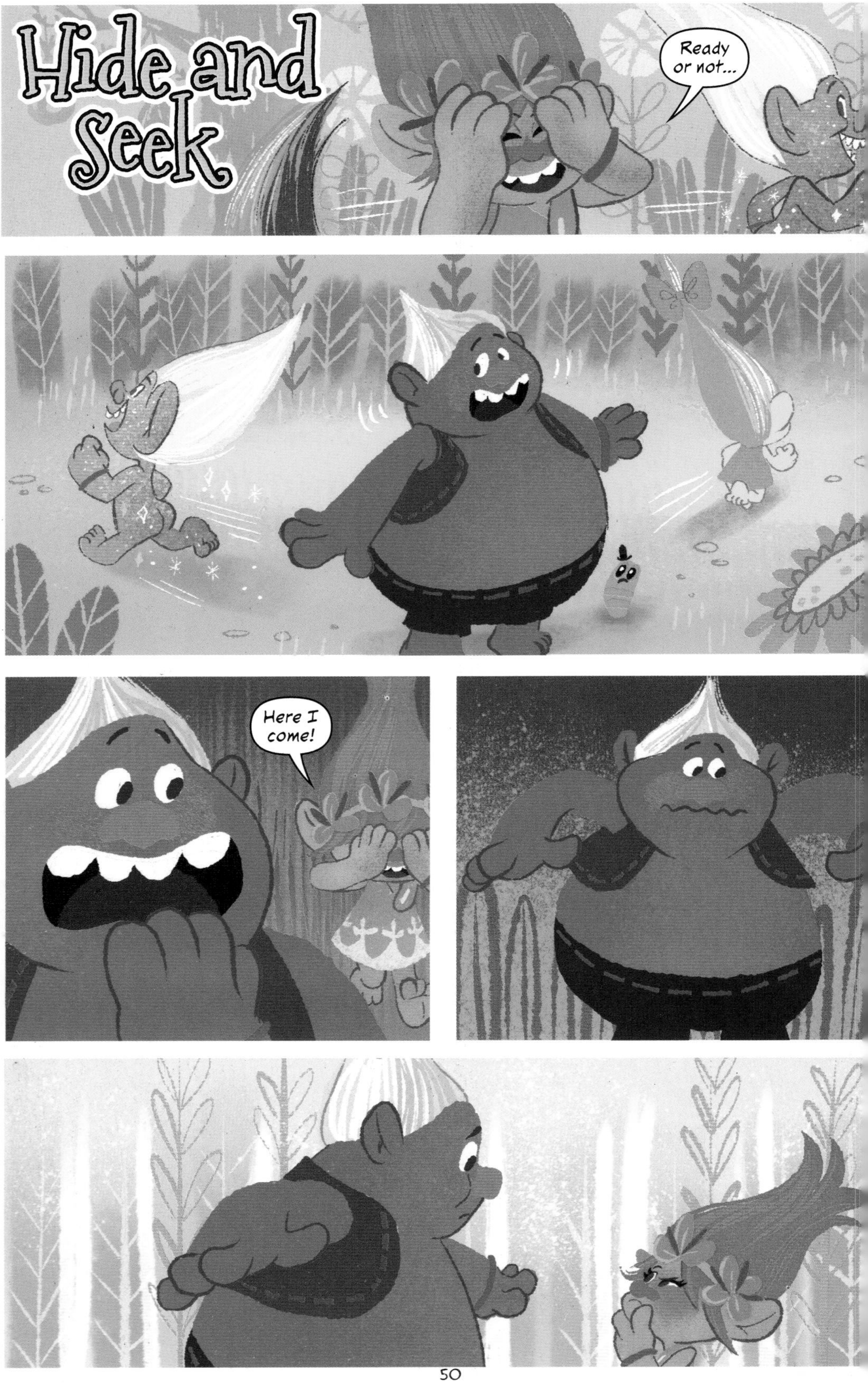
Hide and Seek
Ready or not...
Here I come!

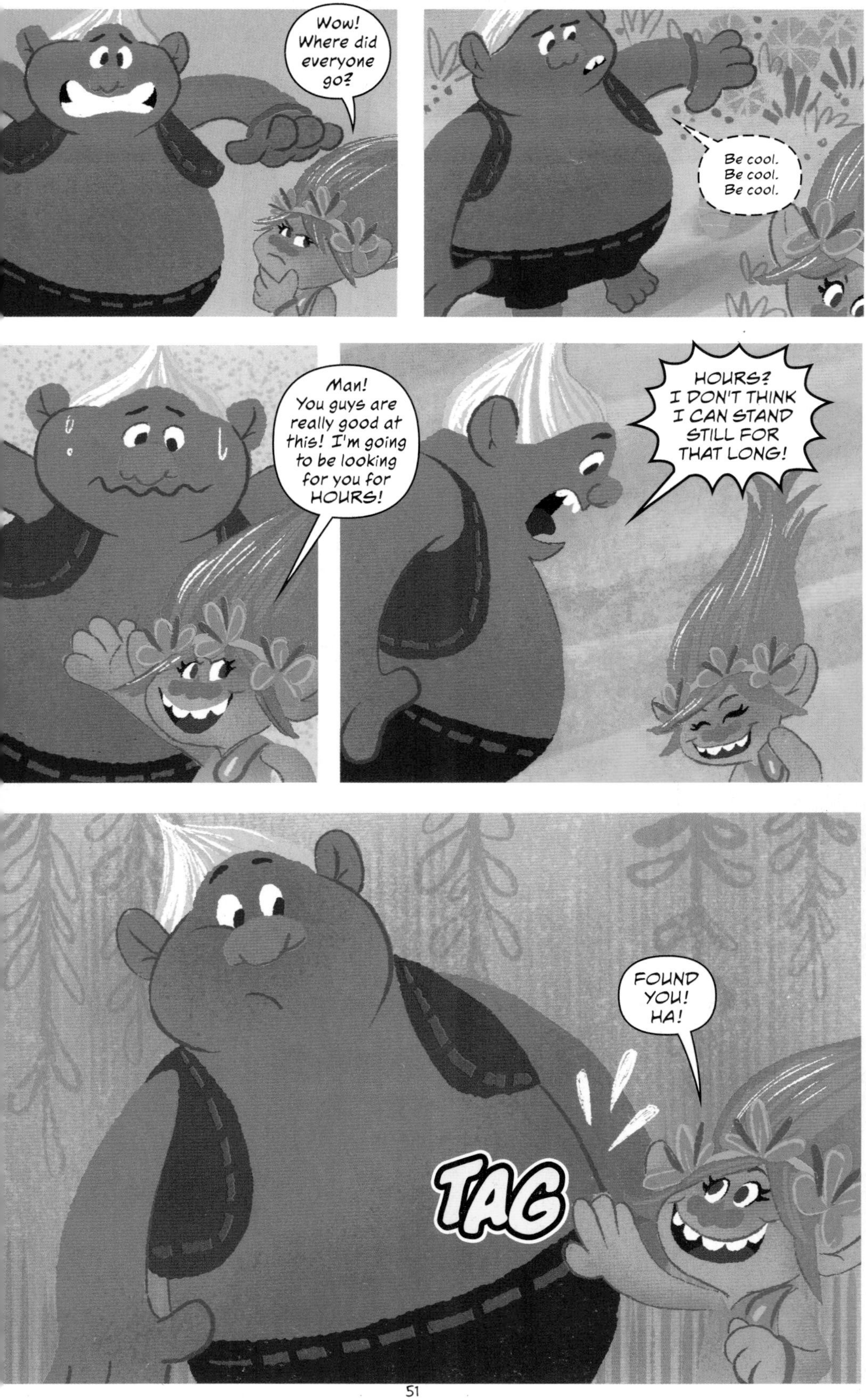
Wow! Where did everyone go?
Be cool. Be cool. Be cool.
Man! You guys are really good at this! I'm going to be looking for you for HOURS!
HOURS? I DON'T THINK I CAN STAND STILL FOR THAT LONG!
FOUND YOU! HA!
TAG

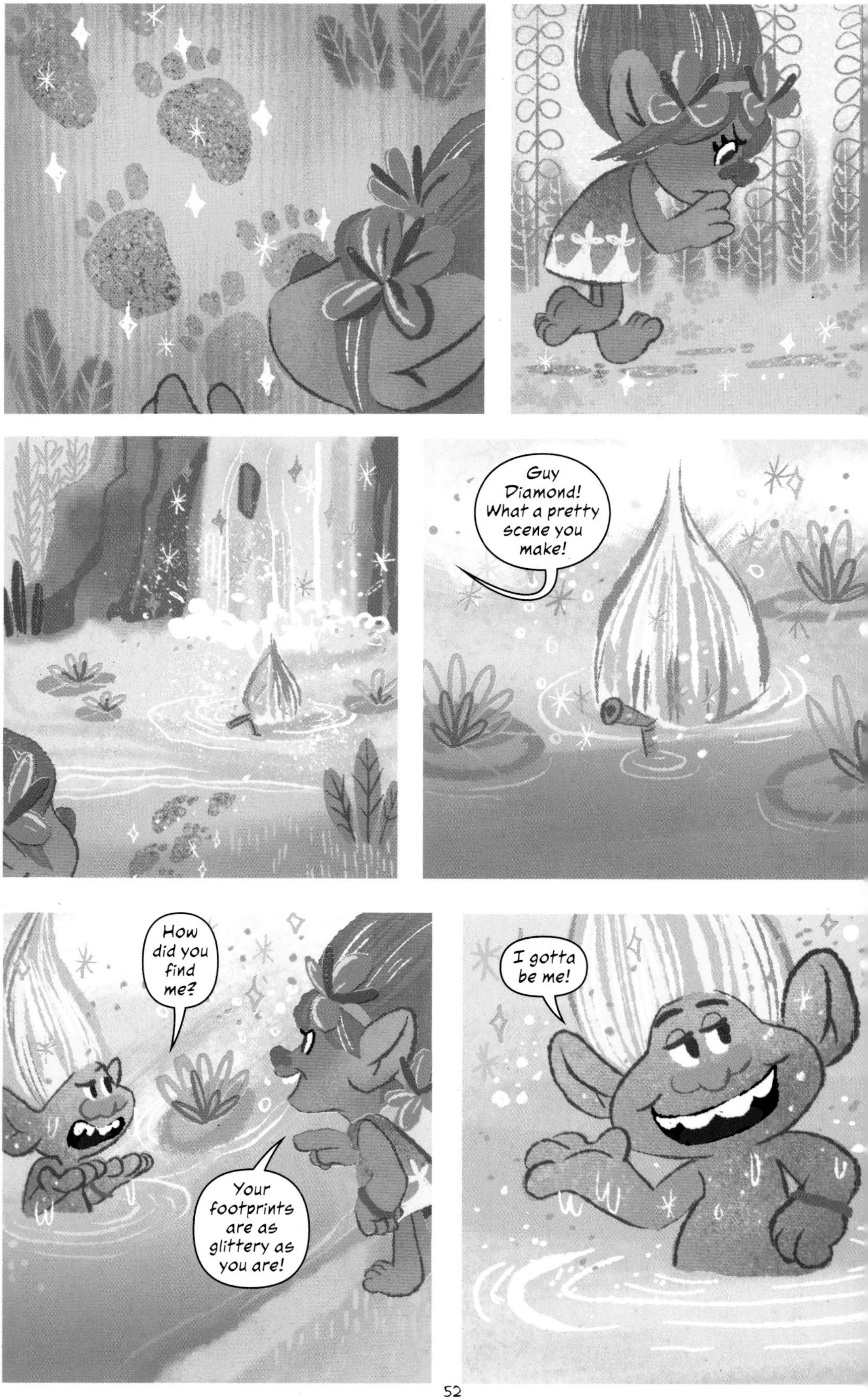
Guy Diamond! What a pretty scene you make!
How did you find me?
Your footprints are as glittery as you are!
I gotta be me!

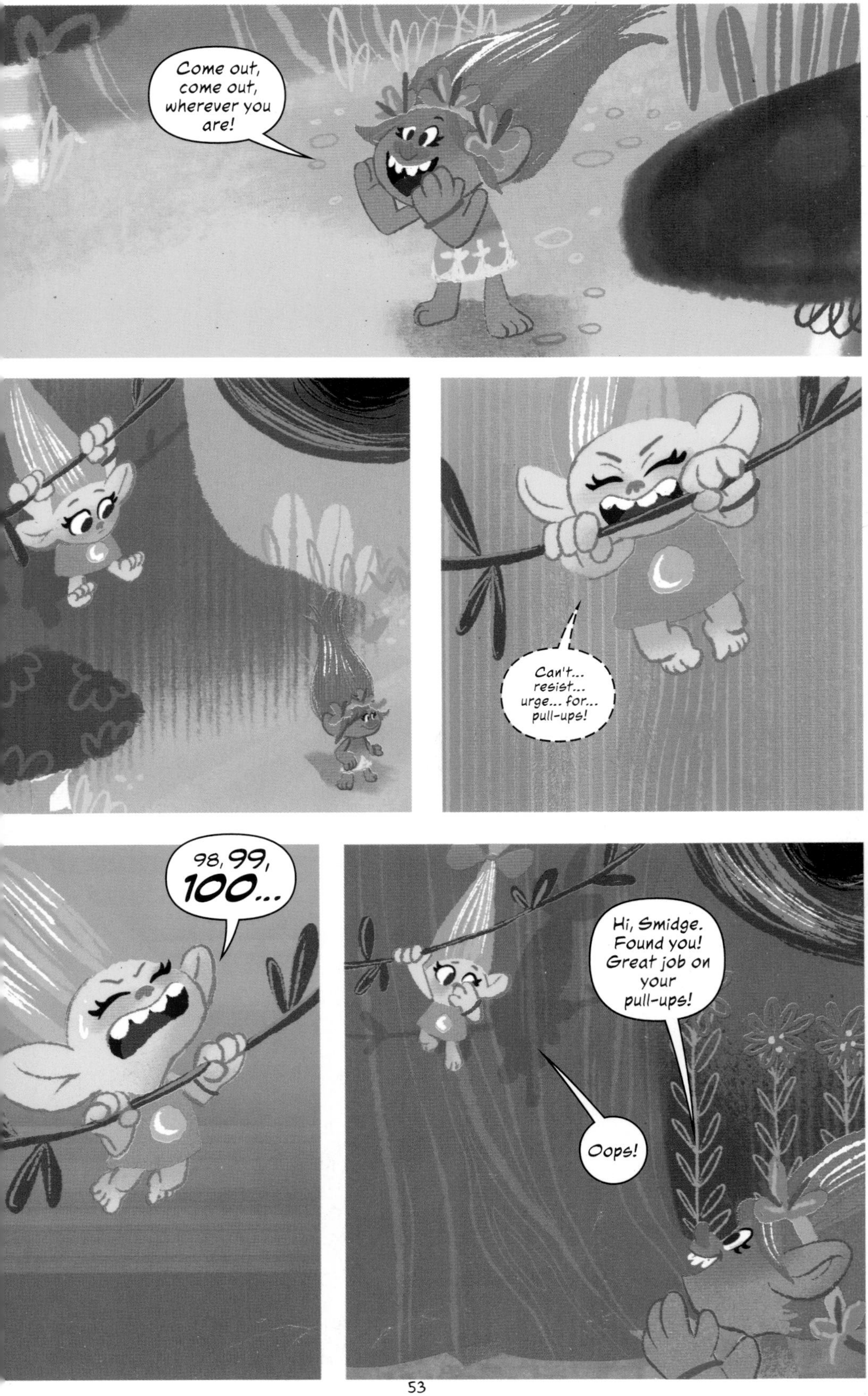
Come out, come out, wherever you are!
Can't... resist... urge... for... pull-ups!
98, 99, 100...
Hi, Smidge. Found you! Great job on your pull-ups!
Oops!

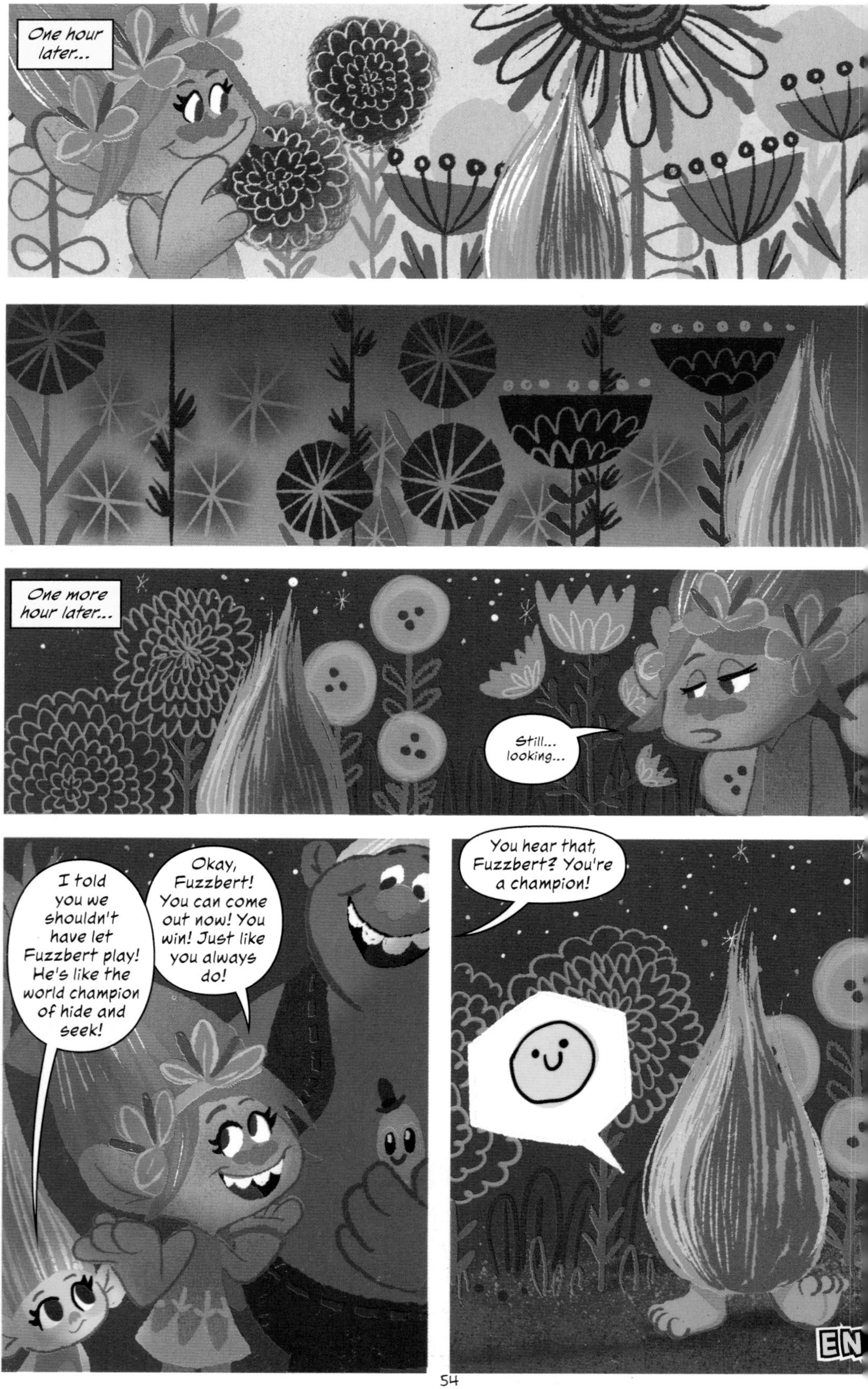
One hour later...
One more hour later...
Still... looking...
I told you we shouldn't have let Fuzzbert play! He's like the world champion of hide and seek!
Okay, Fuzzbert! You can come out now! You win! Just like you always do!
You hear that, Fuzzbert? You're a champion!
END

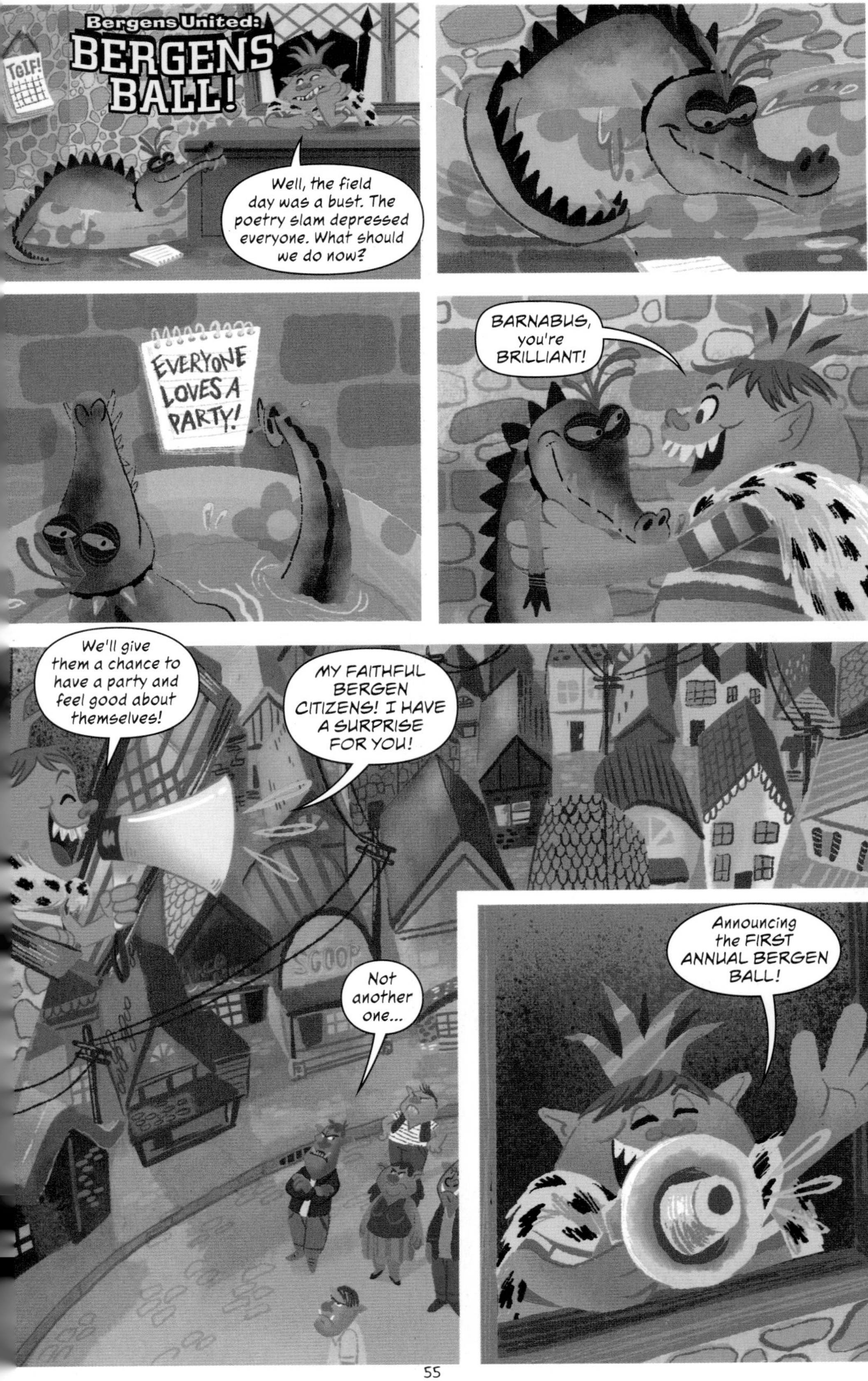
Bergens United:
BERGENS BALL!
TGIF!
Well, the field day was a bust. The poetry slam depressed everyone. What should we do now?
EVERYONE LOVES A PARTY!
BARNABUS, you're BRILLIANT!
We'll give them a chance to have a party and feel good about themselves!
MY FAITHFUL BERGEN CITIZENS! I HAVE A SURPRISE FOR YOU!
SCOOP
Not another one...
Announcing the FIRST ANNUAL BERGEN BALL!

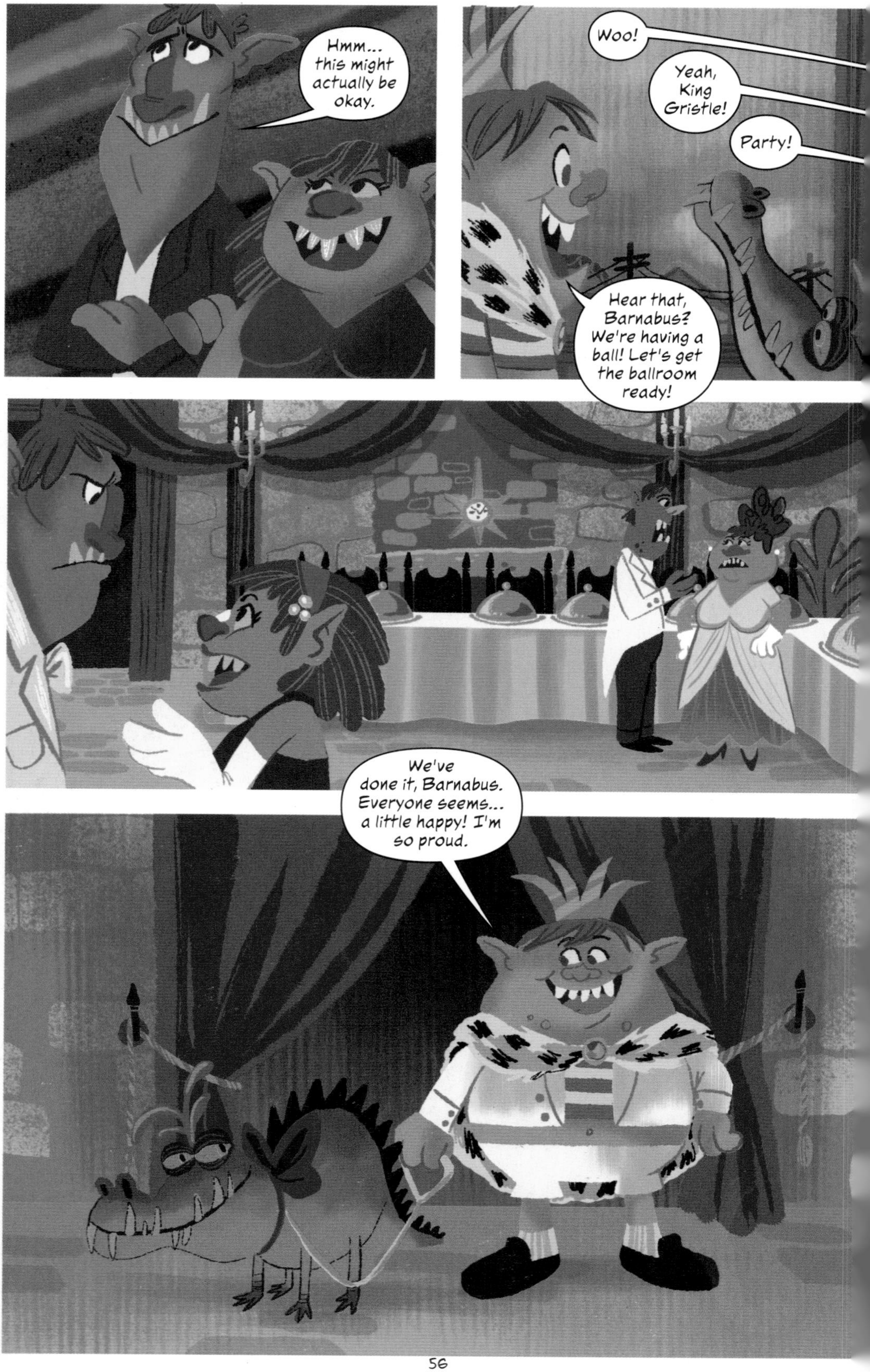
Hmm... this might actually be okay.
Woo!
Yeah, King Gristle!
Party!
Hear that, Barnabus? We're having a ball! Let's get the ballroom ready!
We've done it, Barnabus. Everyone seems... a little happy! I'm so proud.

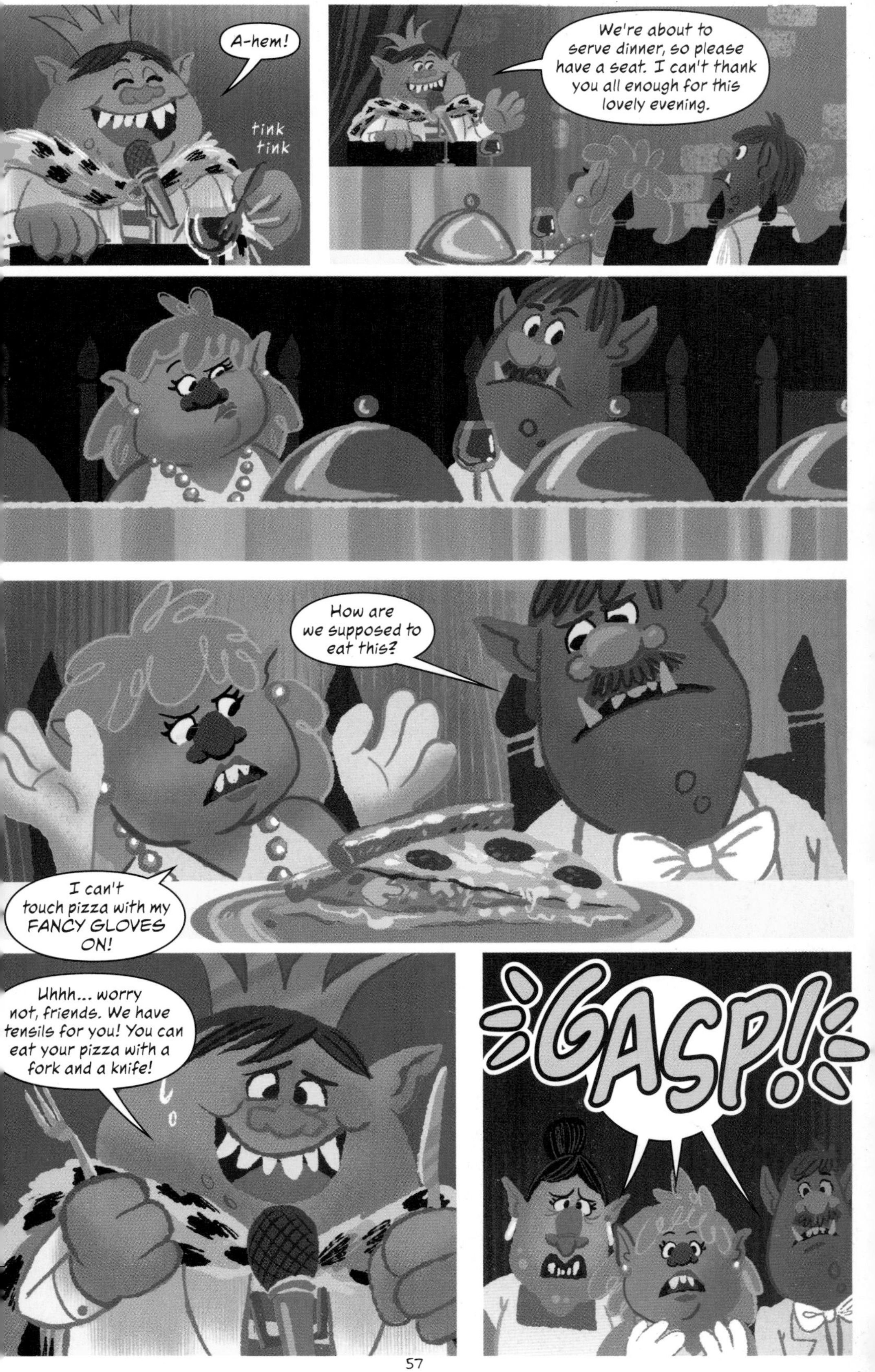
A-hem!
tink tink
We're about to serve dinner, so please have a seat. I can't thank you all enough for this lovely evening.
How are we supposed to eat this?
I can't touch pizza with my FANCY GLOVES ON!
Uhhh... worry not, friends. We have tensils for you! You can eat your pizza with a fork and a knife!
GASP!

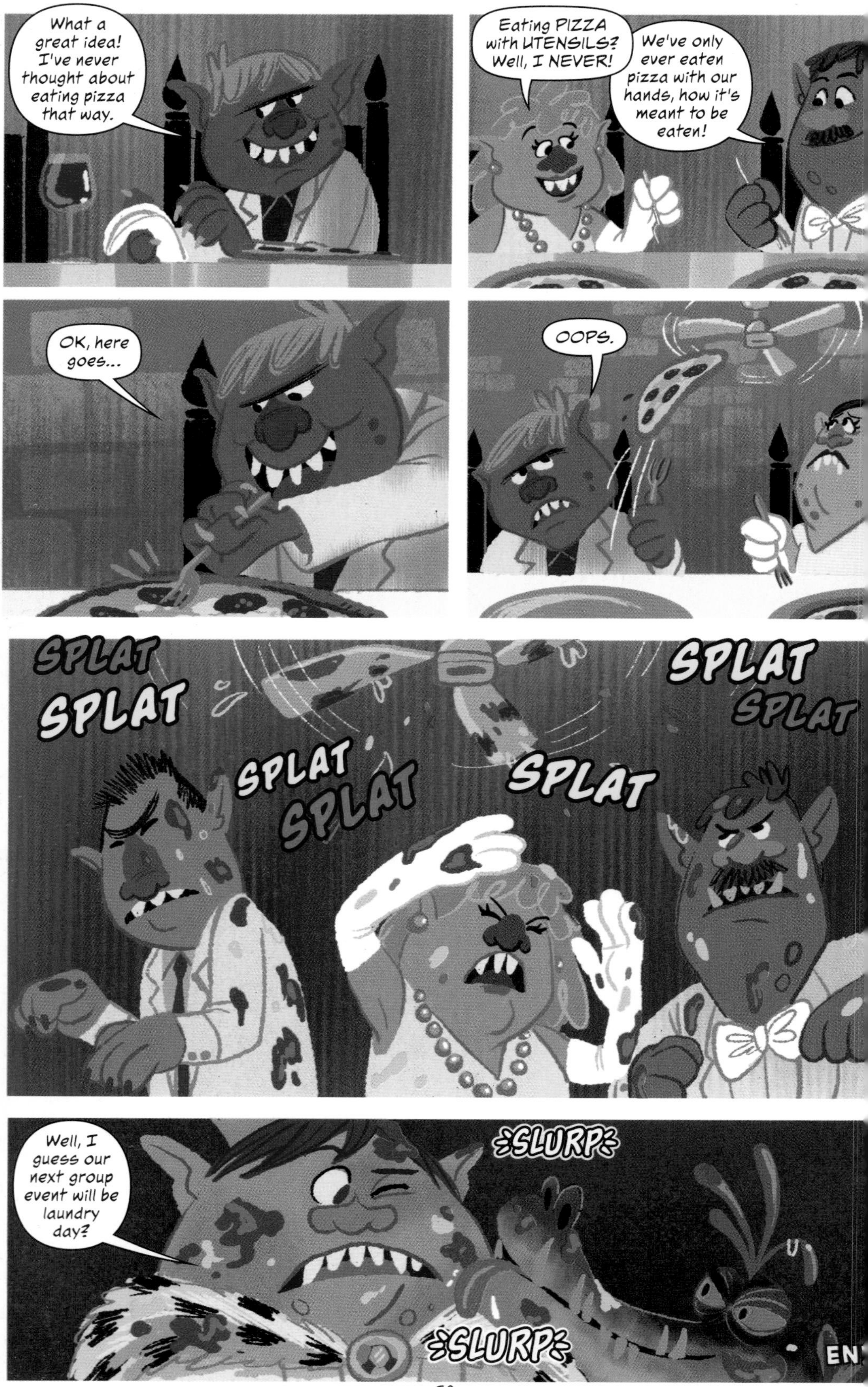
What a great idea! I've never thought about eating pizza that way.
Eating PIZZA with UTENSILS? Well, I NEVER!
We've only ever eaten pizza with our hands, how it's meant to be eaten!
OK, here goes...
OOPS.
SPLAT
SPLAT
SPLAT
SPLAT
SPLAT
SPLAT
SPLAT
Well, I guess our next group event will be laundry day?
SLURP
SLURP
EN

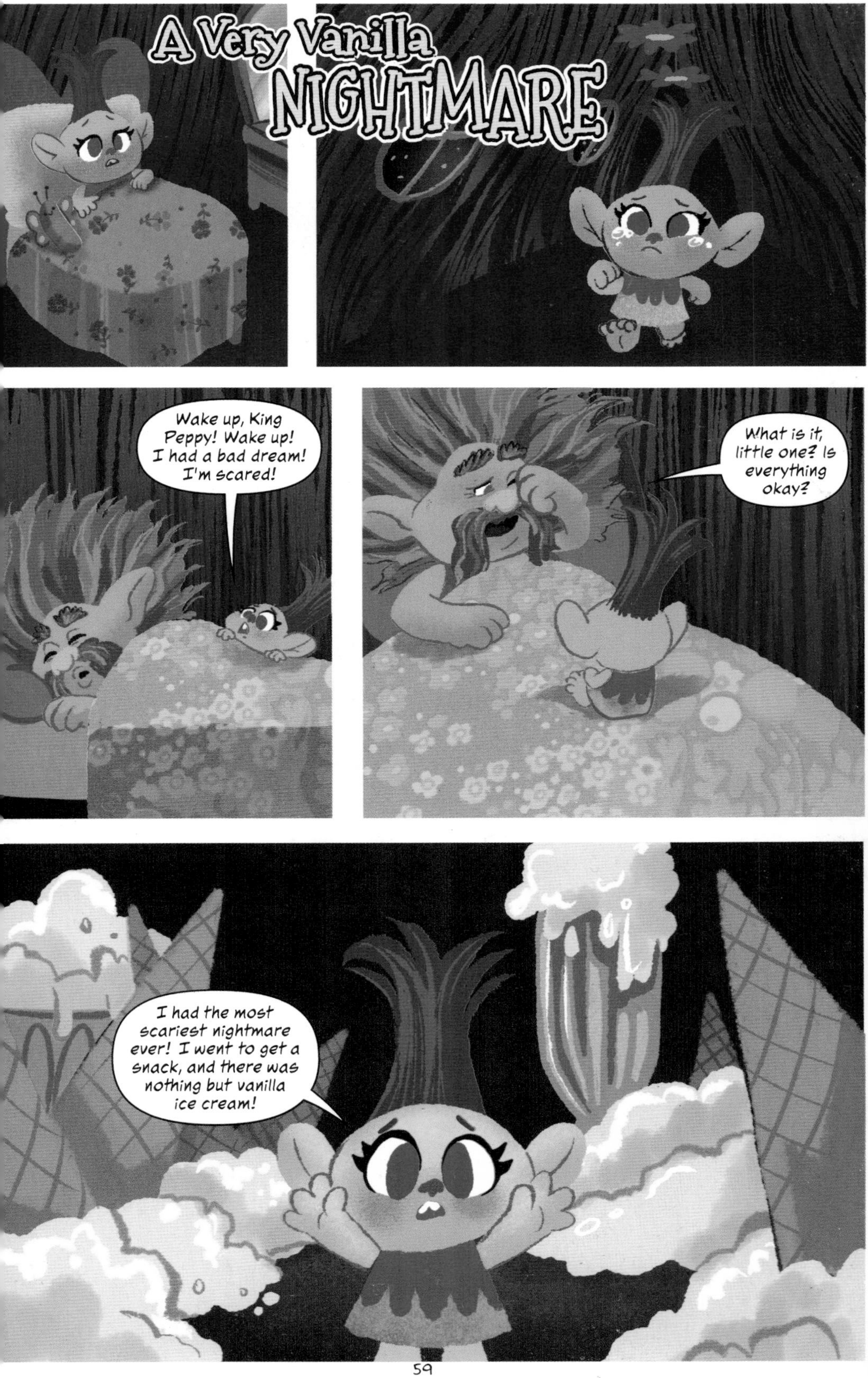
A Very Vanilla NIGHTMARE
Wake up, King Peppy! Wake up! I had a bad dream! I'm scared!
What is it, little one? Is everything okay?
I had the most scariest nightmare ever! I went to get a snack, and there was nothing but vanilla ice cream!

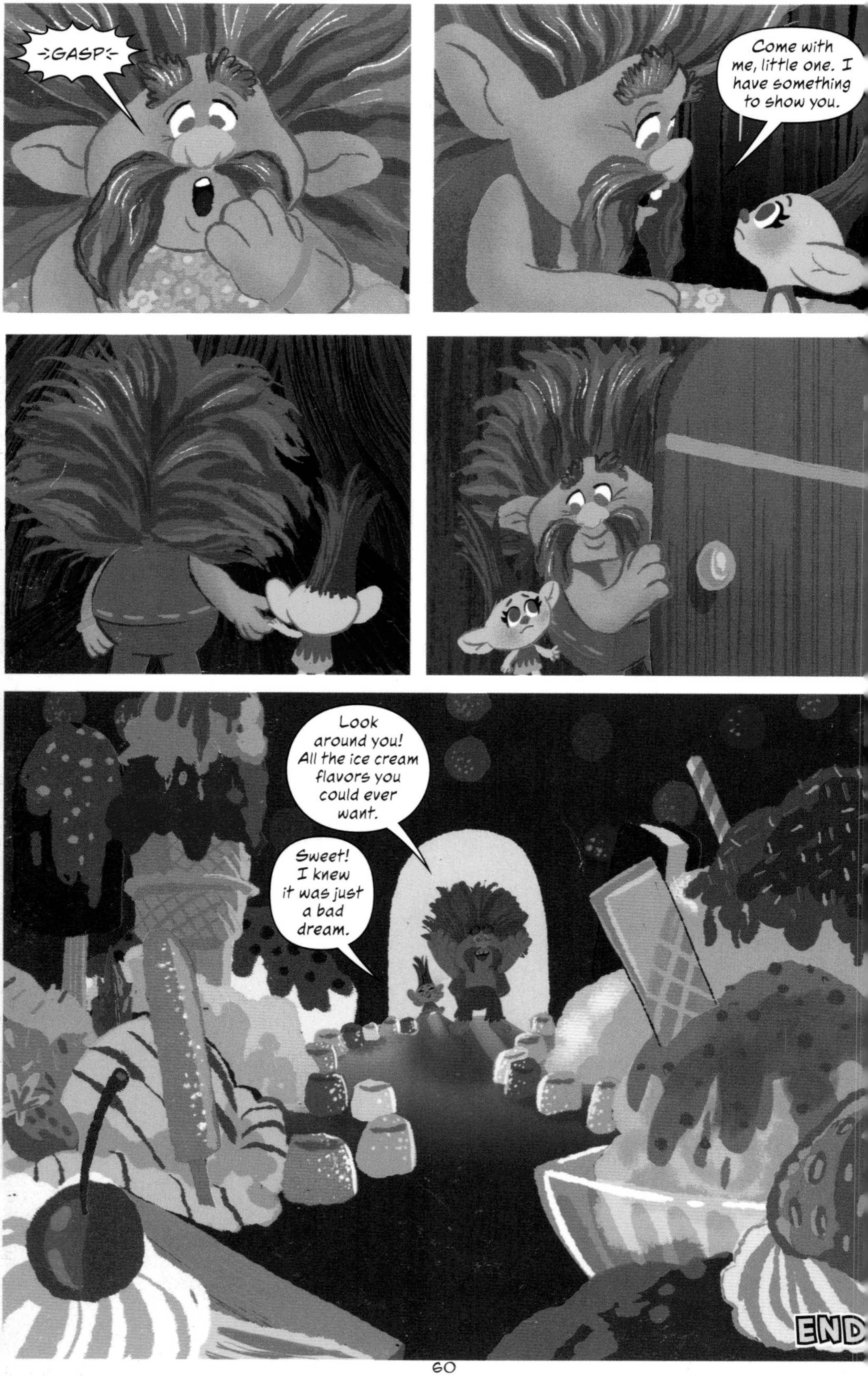

-=GASP=-
Come with me, little one. I have something to show you.
Look around you! All the ice cream flavors you could ever want.
Sweet! I knew it was just a bad dream.
END